Amanda Speedie

# INSIDE OUT

Alex's Story

Published in 2008 by YouWriteOn.com

Published by YouWriteOn.com

# INSIDE OUT

## Alex's Story

## Preface

I knew Alex really well for a few
years when he was in his teens. Well,
I thought I did.

I met him again recently and we got
talking. I told him I write stories now
and he said,

'Write mine.'

So here it is.

Amanda Speedie

This is a true story retold as fiction.
Names have been changed to protect
the feelings of those involved.

1

My dad's really tough. Everyone in my town knows him. He loves the sea.

He's got this big old trawler that he brought back himself from Holland. I don't remember him going to choose it or anything but, next thing, he's home, all knocked about, but with his eyes sparkling, and that old trawler's tied up down at the quay.

There was a bad storm when he brought her back across the channel in the middle of winter. He's standing in our kitchen, smelling of rope and oil, like always, and he says the waves were ten metres high. He says they reared right up above the wheelhouse so that all he could see was a wall of water, then they smashed down onto the boat so she shook.

He keeps laughing. I'm not sure why it's funny, I'm not like him and I don't like going in the water. He thinks I'm a wuss. The sea doesn't scare him though. Nothing does.

He got in a big fight with these three men last summer. He's got these little boats that he rents out to tourists and he had a wooden jetty built, just so they could get in and out without getting their nice shoes wet.

He'd got it in place, all new shiny, and he went down at night to see if it was alright, not rolled away or anything, and in the dark he could see these men messing with it. One of them was bashing at the side trying to break a bit off or something.

I don't know who they were. He didn't know who they were and they can't have known who he was or they'd never have been messing with it.

I'm eating my breakfast and he's telling my mum that he ran down the beach in the dark, grabbed hold of two of them and beat seven bales out of them while the third man ran off yelling for help. I thought that was pretty cool. They shouldn't have been bashing at his stuff.

In the summer I go down to the beach front sometimes to take him some sandwiches that my mum's made. She's not allowed down to the beach front where he's got his hut. He doesn't see me coming at first and I have to climb over a whole load of girls in bikinis. They're sunbathing right outside his hut so I can't get through. He's sitting in a deck chair with a sunhat on, and shades, looking like a cowboy. He doesn't look that pleased when I get there but he says thanks for the sandwiches.

I'm starting senior school soon. My best mate Tommy lives round the corner from me so I see him most days. We kick a ball around in the park, or on the beach sometimes. We go off down the quay once, for a change. I like it round the boats and messy stuff. We're making a noise, just stupid stuff, not doing anything wrong and these two policemen come along.

I don't know what they're talking to us for. We're only kids. We say we're only messing about but they get out their notebooks and ask us what our names are. I say mine and the policeman stops writing and looks at me. 'Are you Greg Marshall's boy?'

'Yes.' He knows my dad.

'Is it your mum that drives that little pink van?'

He must know my mum too.

'You live up on the main road out of town?'

I nod yes at him.

He puts his notebook away. He didn't write anything in it. 'I know your mum,' he says and he nods his head. I'm not sure what he means by this nod. He looks thoughtful, not smiling and not cross with us either.

His voice is different now. He sounds kind. 'You shouldn't be down here, not at night, not in a place like this. Not at your age.' He looks at the other policeman and the other policeman looks at him back. 'It's not a good idea.'

I don't know what he means, and I don't get why they look at each other like that. I can't see what's wrong with messing about down on the quay. My dad's down here most of the time.

Tommy and me walk away, back into town. The two policemen watch us till we're gone round the corner, in case we come back again. I think it's weird. I don't know if I like it that the police know my mum and my dad, and where we live.

There isn't anyone I know in my new class at senior school. My mates have got split up across the year but I don't mind too much. Tommy comes round to call for me before school and we get the bus together. In my class there are other kids who have to come further than me on the bus, and on the train. They have to get up even earlier than me.

The first day is brilliant. I get straight in with this kid from a private school. That's why I'd never seen him around. He's funny. We get on great and we're all messing around. By the time our new teacher comes in it's really loud and we're all over the place. She makes us sit down and be quiet for ages before she starts to say anything. She tells us about the new year and the first day. She's really nice but I think she looks a bit tough too. I like tough people. But that's because I'm not.

My sister's tough too. I'm lucky to have tough people in my house.

Anyway, this old trawler that's Dutch. She's the toughest boat ever. My dad says it didn't matter how big those waves were, that old girl rolled in the troughs and rose up over the crests like a cork floating. And, when they broke right overhead, she popped up through the bubbles, shook herself, and kept right on, heading for England and her new home. He doesn't mind getting knocked about. He doesn't notice little things like bruises.

3

This guy in my class, the one I liked straight off on the first day, is called Jez. I raced him today in lunch break. It was so close I really thought I'd had it, but we got across the field pretty much together. At the last second I reckon we equalized.

Tommy and Dan were watching. Dan said Jez was ahead but Tommy said I won. I'm not sure. I think it was a draw.

I didn't want to be beaten, no way. I didn't want to beat him either somehow. I wanted to win but I didn't want him to lose. Well, not by much, maybe a little bit.

We've got a French teacher who's really old. She looks about fifty. Every time she walks into our classroom she stops and sniffs the air, just like our dog, Scally. She makes a face and says,

'What's that smell?' Sniff. Sniff. 'I can smell something.'

I don't know what we all smell like. It can't be good.

We flop forward on our desks and roll our eyes. She says it every time.

Then she marches over to the windows and throws them all open. It's October.

So we freeze to death in the gale blowing through the windows and don't learn much French.

I've got this idea to catch her out. I tell everyone to bring in stuff that really smells. But kind of nice so she can't complain.

We get in a bit early. Everyone brings something. Jez has some deodorant. Well, he's a bit more man than some of us. He's even got bum fluff on his chin.

Stacey's got some perfume. She says it's some cheap stuff that she found at the back of her bathroom cabinet. She says she didn't dare bring in anything good or her mum would go ape. It stinks. It's really strong and sticky.

There's no perfume in our house. I've got some talcum powder though, so I shake it all over the blackboard rubber and all along the ridge where the teachers leave the chalk.

There's air freshener too and we get busy spraying the curtains, the wooden desks, the air and everywhere, then we sit and wait.

We're so quiet we can hear her footsteps outside. She flings open the door, takes one step in, stops short with a stamp of her feet like a soldier, and stares about.

We're all watching. It's brilliant. She takes a great huge sniff. Her eyes bug out. She jerks her head this way and that, stamps again and says,

'I knew it! I can smell something.'

It's soooooo hard to keep looking blank. There's not a sound. We're all staring at her. I daren't look at Jez or Stacey.

And then she grins. She actually grins. She's a mad old bat but, suddenly, she looks a bit normal, just for a second.

'A ha!' she says. 'Very funny. I can see you're playing a trick on me.'

Now we're all smiling. I like it that she gets the joke. I didn't like her before but I do now.

The smiling stuff doesn't last too long. She's marching over, flinging open the windows and then she gets us all to drag the desks out into the corridor. They're really heavy.

She wants us to own up. I know no-one's going to split on me. They're my friends. Then she says we'll all get detention if the Ringleader doesn't own up.

That's not fair. It isn't everyone's fault. It was my idea. I stick up my hand and say so. She nods. She looks pleased. I can see her point. It's best to tell the truth and I feel better for doing it. I'd hate the others to have a detention because of me.

I see her head jerk to the side. She nods at Jez. I turn round and he's got his hand up too. Then Stacey, then Liam.

It's not horrid. Everyone's laughing. Even me.

Old Smelly Ellie's alright really.

The others get off but Jez, Stacey, Liam and me have to spend all our lunch hour scrubbing perfume out of the wooden desks.

6

The whole school's walking past while we're scrubbing. At first I think I'll feel like an idiot out there with my sleeves rolled up and water and foam everywhere, showing myself up. But I don't. It's the opposite. The Year 11s laugh at us and say,

'Good on yer.'

It's like they like us for it. I feel like I'm famous today and I've only been here for a few weeks. We grin at each other and keep scrubbing.

Mum always wants to go on holiday, for a change, she says.

Dad says, 'Who needs a holiday when we live in a nice place like this?'

There's no money for holidays anyway so Mum says she'll take us camping at half-term with my Auntie Sarah and my cousins. She says I can bring Tommy.

My cousin Ryan got chucked out of three schools. Everyone says he's trouble but I never see it. He's my favourite person in the world. He helps my dad out in the summer down on the beach front, hauling the little boats in and out of the water and taking the money. He's really funny and he can do anything. He's like my sister, Tara. Never scared. They are the two best people ever.

Tommy's great too. He's my best mate. But Ryan's brilliant. I wish he was my brother not my cousin then he could live with us and I'd see him every day. He's the same age as Tara and sometimes I feel like they know stuff I don't. I don't know what their friends are like, not too much anyway, but they both get in a lot of trouble.

Tara and Ryan are bringing a friend each. It'll be cool.

When I wake up on Saturday morning, Mum's already hauled everything outside and she's piling it into the back of her old van. It's full of boxes and a gas stove, a container for water, a kettle and pans. It looks like she's emptied the kitchen into the back of the van.

She's borrowed everything else. I don't know where from. She's got loads of stuff, tents, sleeping bags, everything.

We drive for a bit, all squashed together. The van struggles up long hills and there are trees everywhere, not like by the sea where I live.

We get to this amazing place.

Fat ponies are grazing right by the road. We go slowly past them but they don't even look up, too busy chewing. Massive lumps of granite stick up through the grass and the trees here are small and stubby. When we open the door of the van the air smells all herby.

We carry all the stuff along a path into a flat, grassy space with rusty coloured bracken all around.

Mum looks round. 'Right, she says. 'First we need to choose the best place for the fire.'

She gives the spade to Ryan. 'Next job's for you, Ryan.' She's grinning. She picks up a packet of loo rolls and throws them to Mick.

Ryan and his mate, Mick, have to dig a big hole for a toilet. I didn't think about this and I think Ryan'll be embarrassed. He isn't. He laughs and gets on with it. This is a bit of a yukky thought but, if Ryan doesn't mind, I don't.

Tara's in a strop. 'That's disgusting,' she says. 'I'm not going to use it.'

Auntie Sarah and Mum are putting up the tents. Mum sends Tommy and me off to get a load of wood for the fire. It takes ages. We walk through little winding paths in the bracken. There's pony crap everywhere.

We get to the river. It's fast and deep and it looks brown. I love it. I taste some. It's nice. Really cold.

When we get back to camp the tents are up, Mum's got the kettle on a little gas burner, and Ryan and Mick are making a ring of stones that they've found. Ryan puts some newspaper inside the ring of stones on the grass.

'Hey, Alex,' he says. 'Give us some of the little sticks, mate.'

He balances them round the paper.

'Okay,' he says, 'Now some bigger ones.'

He puts them on top, lights a match and puts it to the paper. It crackles and burns yellow and red. The twigs catch on fire, then the sticks and, last of all, the big bits. It looks brilliant.

He shows me how to keep feeding the fire and says he's going off for a fag and I mustn't tell.

I'd never tell on Ryan.

The sun's gone. It's getting dark and there are tiny stars way up high. I'm not scared of the dark here. The air's cold but the fire's hot. Auntie Sarah's cooked up a pile of potatoes on the little gas stove. Mum's got hot beans and sausages fried in a pan.

We eat round the crackly fire, everyone's faces all smiley, glowing in the dark.

In the night something leans on my side of our tent. It's really big. It's not Mum messing about, even though that's the kind of thing she thinks is funny, scaring people in the dark.

It's definitely not her. It's bigger than a person. I pull away from it a bit and wake Tommy. We can't see anything because it's so dark. There's no room to get closer to Tommy and the thing keeps leaning more and more into our tent till it's going to squash us and the tent flat into the ground.

I think we're going to get mashed.

'What is it?' Tommy's hissing at me.

'I don't know. It's alive though.' It drives me nuts that I don't know what it is.

I'm scared because it isn't making any noise, just slowly pressing its enormous self on top of me. I roll away a bit more. Tommy and me are crushed up together on his side of the tent. Then I think that if I let it, it will squash us to death so I start pushing.

It's like a great big ball. I push and push at it. It stays in the same place. I push some more, shoving hard more than pushing. Pushing doesn't work. I kind of heave at it.

Tommy gets beside me; he heaves and shoves as well. My arms really hurt and I think I've had it but then the walls of the tent suddenly go slack, and it's gone.

Tommy and me don't go to sleep for ages.

In the morning, when we tell the others, they look at us as if we're mad. Mum says there's no herds of cattle up here. Cattle? I thought it was some kind of monster thing. Then I remember the pony crap.

# 3

Tommy and I get sent off to wash the dishes in the river.

Ryan's fiddling with the fire. He calls after us. 'I'll make breakfast while you're gone.'

I can hear Tara making a fuss about the toiletty pit hole thing as we walk away. 'I don't know how you can go in there. It stinks.'

She waits to see which direction we go in and she heads off another way, crashing through the bracken. Trying to find somewhere more ladylike to pee I reckon.

The plastic dishes are cold and the sausage grease is hard with slugs in. I think Tara could come and help. We have to use sand to clean out the pans. The crud won't budge. We don't use it on the plastic. We're not silly.

Mum comes down to the river. She gives us a bucket each. 'I only want the worst off,' and she smiles. 'Give me a hand to carry back some water so we can boil it up.'

When I put my bucket in the water the river is running so fast it's like it wants to yank the bucket right out of my hands and take me with it.

I like washing dishes outside. Ryan's made bacon sandwiches for main breakfast and marmalade sandwiches for pudding breakfast. We sit in the sunshine and drink tea. My hands are warm from the hot dishwater so I feel pretty good.

Ryan's got a big, heavy rope. He ties one end to a tree on our side, then wades across the river with it. I hate watching him. The river's so strong it looks like it's going to knock him over and wash him away. He has to keep stopping. He braces himself against the current, stands still a while, then heads forward again. The water is up to his waist in the middle. He keeps his elbows out for balance.

He gets to the other side, ties the other end to a tree. 'Come on you lot. Get on with it!'

There's an island. I want go over. But I'm afraid of the water.

Mick wades across next, holding the rope as he goes. He slips once or twice but holds on so he's all right. Tara goes over. She's laughing and holding on really tight. She screams sometimes and Ryan calls out, 'You're doing okay, 'and she makes it across.

Her friend, Ally, goes. She looks pretty good. She's steady and quite strong for a girl and she doesn't scream once.

Ryan calls out, 'C'mon, Alex. You next!' but I shake my head. He waves and smiles and then they disappear into the trees on the other side. For a fag I bet.

The next day I find a brilliant tree to climb. It's my secret.

We've lived in three different houses now. Each one has a special tree in the garden where I can hide. The best one was in the last house. When everyone was carrying on I walked down the garden, climbed up onto a big horizontal branch and stayed there. It was my favourite place and no-one knew I was there.

This tree's even bigger.

It's at the side of a clearing. The leaves are turning rusty and brown and the sun has it all lit up.

I bring the heavy rope from camp and go off to the clearing. Tommy's busy making a dam at the side of the river. No-one sees me go.

It takes me a few minutes to work out the best way to climb up. There aren't any low branches. I put the coil of rope over my head and under one arm like I've seen the mountaineers do, and begin to climb up. I find footholds and handholds, even though some are a bit of a stretch. I get really high up.

A long branch stretches out across the clearing. It's perfect. I get astride it and shuffle along out to the middle. I'm going to go down, slow and controlled, hand over hand on the rope. I'll land soft like a parachutist on the earth floor underneath.

I sit on the branch. I have to get my breath back a bit. It's nice and cool up here.

It takes a while sorting out my knots. I make the rope really secure around the branch. Then I tie the other end round my middle. I think I've got it tight enough.

And then I jump.

I fall really fast, out of control.

The ground rushes up and, with a great yank, the rope runs out.

I feel like I've bust my ribs. It hurts a lot. The knot that was round my middle has got yanked up into my ribcage. It's cutting in, really tight.

My feet aren't touching the ground.

I hang there for a minute, thinking what I need to do next.

Then I hear voices.

Ryan and Mick appear through the bracken. They're talking and they don't see me at first.

Ryan stops and stares at me. He looks at me for just a second, as if he's weighing things up.

'Are you okay?'

I try to look kind of casual. 'Yeah. Sure.'

He steps forward. 'Do you want a hand to get down?'

'No. I'm fine. I'll just hang here for a bit.'

I really do want to get down, and my ribs hurt like crazy. I don't want him to have to help me down though, like I'm stupid.

He looks a bit doubtful so I move my arms around and say, 'So, what you two doing then?'

'We're off to the pub. It's over there somewhere.' He waves an arm.

'Oh, right.' I say.

They trudge off. I can't imagine there's a pub, house or anything up here on the moor. But, if there is one, Ryan'll find it.

He looks back over his shoulder at me with a frowny face so I wave and smile.

'Be back this afternoon,' he says, and they disappear again into the bracken on the other side of the clearing.

I hang there for a bit. I feel like an idiot but I reckon I convinced him.

I have a go at loosening the knot in front of my chest. It's really difficult because the rope's so tight but, after ages, and when my fingers are really sore, I get it loose and fall down onto the ground.

It's okay to lay there for a minute because no-one's looking. I hurt too much to climb up again to get the other end down.

We use it for a rope swing later.

## 4

I've only got my school stuff so I don't go and see people much the rest of the time. I feel a bit stupid in my school clothes. I've got these jeans but they're half way up my ankles now and I've got one shirt that nearly fits. The sleeves are too short but that's not so bad.

Mum says I should ask my dad for some money for Christmas. 'He'll say no if I ask,' she says.

I have to be smart and choose my moment. He's sitting in the chair looking alright so I go over and say can I ask him something. He smiles all pleased, 'Of course. What is it?'

He likes me. Because I'm a boy. I know that. He doesn't like Tara. If he sees her he snarls at her, 'What are you hanging around the house for?' She keeps out of his way.

When I ask him there's a moment when I feel frightened. I don't know why. He's never hurt me. Not ever. He did shout at me once, when I was six. It scared me so much I ran away. I went quite a long way but it was all right because Scally came with me so I wasn't lonely.

He narrows his eyes at me and leans back in his chair. He stares at me as if I'm different from just a minute ago. I feel different. He's weighing me up. It seems like for ages.

Then he asks, 'How much?'

I know he's going to want detail. He's got that kind of summing up look on his face, so I list what I need, new trousers, new T-shirts and a sweatshirt, some new shoes for outside school. Then I make a guess at a figure. He stares at me some more, sits forward and says,

'Okay.'

But he halves the figure I said.


Mum's angry. She's all red in the face but too angry for crying. She only cries if she's sad. She puts all the stuff for the Christmas dinner on the table and says, 'We'll eat without him,' and she bashes about in the kitchen.

My dad comes in all smiles and stinking, rubs his hands. 'I love Christmas,' he says all slurry and he sits down and picks up his knife and fork.

My mum's roast dinners are brilliant. Dad's paper hat slips off all the time and his eyes are red.

Mum smiles but she looks like she's pretending. Tara stares at her plate. I want to go to my room.

This time it's okay. He's making an effort because it's Christmas.

We get back to school after Christmas and I feel like I've been at this school for years even though it's only my second term. We have Maths first. Our Maths teacher's really harsh. Really serious. I don't actually remember him being harsh or doing anything harsh, I just reckon he is harsh. He looks like he would be. None of us ever push our luck. He's not that kind of teacher. He teaches us stuff and we sit quiet. I love Maths. I'm really good at it.

Jez is really good at Maths. I keep looking over to see what mark he gets for his homework and he leans over to check what I get. We're pretty much the same most days. Well, okay, he sometimes get a bit better mark than me, but not always.

We're all being quiet, and waiting for Mr Dryden to get going and he doesn't say anything. So we watch him and he looks round at all of us, very slowly, like he's never seen us before. Then he says,

'Isn't there someone in this class called Marshall?'

I stare. I'm not sure what I've done. I don't remember doing anything. I think it must have been something really bad if he's going to embarrass me in front of everybody. I can feel Stacey looking at me. She's on the desk by my right shoulder but I can feel her look at me, without turning round to check.

He's still looking round. He looks a bit frowny and I can't tell if he's cross. I stick my hand up, not very high, only a bit so no-one will notice too much, and say,

'That's me, Mr Dryden.'

He smiles at me. Weird. I've never seen him smile. He looks different when he's smiling.

'Ah.' He says. 'So would your father be Greg Marshall?'

Oh no, I'm thinking. Who's he beat up now? And I don't answer but I nod, just a bit, not too obvious, and my neck's burning because I know everyone's staring.

Why does Mr Dryden have to pick on me in front of my mates?

'He had quite a weekend, didn't he?'

Did he? I don't know. I don't see him much. He's always at sea. Or down the pub.

I just stare at Mr Dryden. And he's still smiling.

'Yes.' He says. 'He's a brave man. You must be very proud.'

I don't get it.

And then he gets out this newspaper, smoothes it across with his hand and reads aloud.

It's only the headline. I'm glad he doesn't read the whole thing.

He says, 'Trawlerman puts to sea to save stricken vessel.' He looks up at me.

'And the lifeboat wouldn't go out because it was too rough,' he adds, and looks at me again.

I'm just blinking. I don't get it. Everyone's muttering and stuff and I can feel Stacey again. It's like her eyes are hot on me. I feel happy but I don't speak. I smile though.

'You didn't know?' he says. His eyebrows go up to make a question and I shake my head no.

Mr Dryden folds the paper, puts it to one side and cracks on with the lesson.

I feel different today. Centre of attention for a bit. It's nice. When I get home, Dad's there. He isn't usually. So I ask him what happened with the boat but he doesn't say much. 'I got a line on it and towed it in, that's all,' he says.

Next day I get hold of a copy of the weekly paper that Mr Dryden had. I was going to show my dad but the bad weather's settled and he's gone again, back to sea.

I read,

Local skipper Greg Marshall put out to sea alone in his trawler, the *Pearl* on Tuesday night. Winds were gusting forty knots and the swell was running at five metres. The lifeboat crew had mustered but Coxswain, Mike Burrows, made the decision not to launch because conditions were too bad.

'It was a tough call,' he said. 'It was too dangerous on the bar to risk the lives of the crew. I didn't think we'd be able to reach the vessel or go alongside in that sea. Mr Marshall was extremely brave in the circumstances, particularly to put to sea alone. I take my hat off to him.'

The owner and crew of the stricken vessel, the *North Star*, are safely ashore and there is only minor damage to the boat. Mr Marshall has said he will not be claiming salvage.

I feel my eyes bug out when I read this. On his own? I try to imagine my grumpy dad in the pub, hearing there's something up, going off down to the harbour side. Maybe he stands in the rain watching the *North Star* surging about in boils over the bar with no engine and no way to get in, and seeing they aren't going to make it.

He wouldn't have run. I've never seen him run, but he's quick somehow. I see him go off down to the quay, long strides, jaw set, eyes glinty. He climbs aboard in the dark, starts up the engine, casts off, and takes his tough little Dutch girl out into the storm. He knows she will make it.

He gets out through the breakers, so big they would crush any other little boat, but not the *Pearl*.

He gets as close as he dares and now, he has to come out of the wheelhouse, one man, muscle and bone, out in the screaming storm.

I think he could be washed away, knocked over clean into the scuppers and out at the stern. But no, he takes a rope, the biggest, heaviest rope, makes a monkey's fist at one end, and throws it to the crew of the *North Star*.

They're lined up on the deck staring into the black night. Do they catch it the first time or does it fall in the water so he has to try again? No-one's in the wheelhouse so the *Pearl*'s got no master, but she's patient.

The crew catch the line and tie it on. The wind is screaming around their ears. The bow of their fishing boat points up to the moon one minute, then nosedives down into the sea the next. They don't fall off.

My dad gets back in his wheelhouse that stinks of damp and mould and old oil, puts the strong old donkey engine in gear, spins the wheel and tows the *North Star* in.

The lights of the two boats shine through the dark. The lifeboat men wait on the quayside in their big jumpers. The huddled watchers on the quayside, and all along the promenade, hug their arms to themselves and try to keep warm.

My dad can't see them. He's concentrating.

I like having a hero for a dad.


A while after, my mum's fluttering about trying to choose a dress. My sister and me have to go and stay with my cousins for a couple of days because Mum and Dad are going to Buckingham Palace.

I think Dad's going to meet The Queen but he doesn't. He meets a politician though. 'He shook my hand,' he says. 'He was very nice.' That's all he said about it.

The politician gave him a big wooden barometer for bravery. I try to imagine a politician in a suit shaking hands with my scratchy old dad.

I can't.

Dad's really proud of the barometer. I can tell. It's got his name on it.

We keep it on the wall in our dining room where you can see the sea from the windows. Mum reckons it was a captain's house a hundred years ago because you can see the sea from windows on three sides of it. Not from my room though. My room's at the back facing the road, and the roof slopes down onto the sheds where Dad keeps a load of gear.

I like my room a lot. I hate this house though.


I hated it the minute I stepped in it.

Mum was really excited about moving. I had to go to school in the morning from my old house and come home to this place, on the bus. That was last year, in Year 6.

I liked it on the bus. My sister, Tara, was waiting at the bus stop when I got off, so she could show me where the new house was, but it wasn't far.

I couldn't see it at first. There was only a door in a long wall along the road. I thought that was weird. I couldn't see above the wall because I'm not very tall; I could only see the wall and a black painted door so it looked like a secret.

Tara opened the door and it creaked. The hinges were rusty and salty. She shoved it hard because it was so stiff, and it was a shock. I didn't expect it. Right in front of me, level with my eyeballs, was the horizon. The sea was all shimmering and sparkly and went on forever. The breeze off the sea smacked me in the face and hit me in the throat so I couldn't speak.

The door banged back against the rail and Tara stuck her arm out so I didn't fall forwards. A huge flight of concrete steps went down in front of us. You could stare at the sea and fall down the steps if you didn't know they were there.

The house is built under the road and right above a railway line. Seriously weird. It looks okay from outside. I hate it inside.

I stand in the middle of the sitting room. There's boxes everywhere, bits of newspaper spilling all out. Mum's got all glistery eyes, she's so excited, and I hate it. I really hate it. I feel like bad things happen here.

My mum loves the sea. When I wake up in the mornings she's always outside, in her dressing gown, sitting on the low wall in front of the house, staring at the sea, looking all dreamy. She's never been to sea though. Dad doesn't let her near the boat or the quay.

## 5

My sister's cool. She's three years older than me but it seems like more than that. She's not at my school because she got chucked out of there. She's at one in this town so she doesn't have to get the bus home like I do.

Tara's cool because she's never scared.

At my last school, at primary, this new kid joined. He had a face like a gorilla's bum. That wasn't his fault I suppose, but he was an idiot. He said he'd been to loads of city schools and that we were retards down here. I said he had to keep moving schools because he was a retard. He said he'd get me for that.

He didn't get me, not then, so I didn't know when he'd get me. I started looking out for him. I told Tara so she skived off school to come and meet me outside mine for a few days.

It's okay. She doesn't go to her school much anyway but I don't tell my mum that.

'I want to have a look at him,' she said. 'See if he's worth bothering about.'

She waited outside for me. When I came out he walked by. She looked at him like she meant it. She didn't show me up by saying anything to him. She stood close by him, stared hard, up, down, right in his face.

I saw him check her out. I could tell then that it was okay. She doesn't look scary, not exactly. Pretty, but scary.

On the bus home she said, 'He's all mouth, he won't touch you.'

She got chucked out of my school - where I am now - for fighting, even though she was only sticking up for her mate. She always sticks up for people. She said no-one would touch her family, certainly not gorilla-bum-face. And he left me be.

I know I said I hate the house but I like my room. Tara likes it because of the sloping roof down from the window. She wakes me up sometimes when she opens the door and comes into my room.

She says, 'Shush. I'm just sneaking out.'

She opens my window, sticks one leg out, lifts herself over the sill, and she's gone.

I wake up when I hear her scratching about on the tiles, like they could slip off, so I know she's come back.

She says she meets her mates out in the road and they walk about. It's cold though, and she sees them in the day. I think Ryan does it too. I don't know why.

I try it one night. I climb out and go round to Tommy's house. When I get there I think he's forgotten I'm coming and he's asleep, so I stand outside in his garden. I throw bits of grit up at his window till he looks out.

He struggles a bit getting out of his bedroom window onto the flat roof of the back porch. It's further down than it looks. We try to be quiet but you can't be quiet when you're laughing.

When we get out of his garden and onto the road we're not sure where we should go. We wander round for a bit but we get bored so we go home. The only fun bit is trying not to get caught. Nobody even knows we're out here wandering about so there's no point. I don't know why Tara bothers.

6

My mum tried to teach me to swim. Tara can do it really well. I can't see why they like it. It goes in your face and up your nose till you choke. Mum tries to be patient. I only notice that when she stops. 'For goodness sake,' she says. 'I give up.' She stomps off, back up the beach.

I stay in the water. Waves slap into me. I feel stupid. I hate it. I can't help it if I'm rubbish in the water.

Anyway, I'm good at other things. So.

Scally and me run along the beach. Scally can run even faster than me. He runs along with his tail up and his mouth open so he looks like he's grinning. I throw sticks for him and he chases after them and brings them back.

He's only trying to please me really. He's not a pet. He's his own dog, so it's nice of him to keep me company.

Everyone in the town knows Scally too. He's not at home much either. No-one is.

Our next door neighbour's a bachelor man, a sailor. He says Scally comes round to call for him so they can go to the pub together. He says Scally comes through a hole in the fence, runs round outside the house so old Bill can see him out of the window. Then he sits and waits at the back door till Bill comes out.

I can't imagine Scally in a pub. I don't see how that's much fun for a dog.

I never see my mum put food down for him. He goes out and gets his own, comes back with a bone sometimes. He raids peoples' bins too. Mum gets really mad at him for that because he smells bad and does terrible farts. He looks sad like his tummy hurts but she's still cross. Poor Scally.

When I was really small, in the first year at primary, I walked to school. Everyone got there around the same time. The mums all walked us in.

One day we came round the corner to the school and Scally was there. I jumped forward and called to him but my mum caught hold of me and yanked me back.

'Shush,' she said. 'Keep walking.'

She looked so uncomfortable I didn't understand. I wanted to get Scally. He's ours.

When we got closer, I could see other mums hurrying their kids into the school. The kids were trying to stare at Scally and our school dog, Bessie.

They looked weird. They were stuck together, back to back. Scally had such a sad and worried look on his face. I didn't know how they'd got stuck together like that, bum to bum, like Siamese dogs. I opened my mouth to say something kind to him. Mum pulled me into the school yard.

She hissed at me, 'Don't say he's ours.'

I guessed then. I didn't know what he and Bessie had been doing before we got there, but somehow I did now. I couldn't see what was wrong with it. I thought it was nice that he loved Bessie. I didn't like it that he looked so unhappy though.

Our teacher, Miss Smith, took us to see the pups a bit later. I wanted one. They were half mine anyway, but I knew I mustn't say so.

So Scally and me run on the beach. If he's not around I go down there on my own. I don't see Tommy after school. His parents watch him do his homework.

I do mine. I just do it by myself, then I go out. I don't like it in this house. I don't know if it's worse when it's empty or when everyone's shouting.

I feel safe outside, on the beach.

I don't feel safe at home.

## 7

The railway line cuts our house off from the beach. If it wasn't there we could run down the garden, through the tamarisk at the bottom of the slope and down onto the sand. It would be steep but we'd make a track.

There's an old, wooden bridge a short way away, a couple of minutes at a run, but it's broken. You can climb the steps but that's all. The bridge rotted long ago. Before I was even born. The only way to the beach is the long way round, by the road. What a waste of time.

I run down the garden, out of the bottom gate, and climb over the wall onto the railway line. The stones are all dirty yellow and rusty brown. I can't see any poo or paper between the rails so it's not true that train toilets spit out underneath the carriages or there'd be stinky mess everywhere. It looks filthy though.

I look up and down. Can't see anything coming. I listen for the hiss on the metal. If I hear hissing I climb back out of there onto the path under our garden and wait.

No hissing. Can't see a train. Safe to run. Jump over the metal rails. Mustn't touch them in case they're live and I get electrocuted.

I'm scared but it's good scared. Up to me to time it right.

It's harder getting up onto the wall on the other side because the top of it is near my neck. I have to jump so I land on my chest on top of it first. No-one's seen me so I won't get in trouble. There's a big sign,

NO TRESPASSING ON THE RAILWAY LINE

I heave myself over, drop onto the sea wall, run down the nearest set of steps, and I'm on the beach.

I run along it, just for the hell of it. The sea smells clean. The waves suck the sand, drool it out again and roll back. I like it down here. I never get caught. I'm too quick.

Tara's mad. She runs through the tunnels. I'd never do that. Long, dark tunnels. So long you can't see the light at the other end. I know because I've been on the train.

The only way to get to Shell Cove is by boat. Sometimes she goes that way, if one of her friends borrows one. But they can't all get in it anyway. They load up the boat with cider and fags, and sleeping bags, and stay over there all night.

'If a train comes when you're in the tunnel,' she says. 'It'll suck you underneath.'

She looks very strict when she teaches me things. 'You have to lie down, between the track and the wall,' she says. 'Press yourself flat to the gravel, cling to the ground somehow, and stick yourself down till it's gone.'

No way.

I like the idea of sleeping out on a secret beach where no-one can find you. No-one fighting and being mean. Just you and your friends talking, messing about, laughing. Sitting by a beach fire, stars above your head, cold sand and the sea gently lapping at the shore.

But I can't get to that place.


The big boys are nice to me on the bus. They know Tara so they think I'm all right. They sit on the back seat and smoke. They fight sometimes, but they don't mean it. Tommy and me had a cigarette one day. When I get in the kitchen Mum's home. She sniffs at me and says, 'You stink. Have you been smoking?'

'Eugh. No,' I say, making a twisty face. 'The big boys were though. I hate it. It stinks.'

I feel really bad for lying.


My Auntie Sarah and Mum are planning another holiday. We're going to a Youth Hostel this time. I'd rather go camping. Ryan's not coming. He's gone to some young offender's place, Tara says. I don't know what he's done but Mum and Auntie Sarah go all whispery if anyone says his name.

Tommy can't come. He's got a cold.

I can't believe it. I have to go in the same sleeping room with Tara and her friend, my mum and my auntie.

I want to go in the men's sleeping room on my own but they say no. I feel such an idiot.

My mum keeps farting, all night. I won't laugh because I'm mad with her. But I do after a bit.

We laugh all night and she still keeps farting. 'I can't help it,' she says but she doesn't look sorry. People complain and we get told off by the warden for making too much noise.

We walk miles up and down hills. They're quite pretty I suppose, but it's not fun without Ryan. I wish I could go and visit him.

## 8

My dad's not home much, but that's good because he's so grumpy.

I came home from school yesterday, really hungry. I'm always starving. And he was in the kitchen.

The air crackled when I walked in.

I wanted to go to the fridge and see if there was any food in it. I always do that even though I know there won't be. Sometimes I find some biscuits, if the bread and cake man had just called round in his van.

Yesterday, though, I couldn't go to the fridge because my dad was leaning on it. Mum was one side with her face all frowny and my dad was the other. He's really tall. He had his arm across it like he was hugging it, or holding it somehow, while he half lay across the top.

They didn't notice me.

Mum kept saying, 'Please,' but he wasn't saying much, just mumbling something. I couldn't hear what Mum said, she was speaking so low, but she looked like she meant it.

My dad made a big noise, a sort of groaning sigh, straightened up and put his hand in his pocket. His jeans were tight and his fingers went white when he forced them in, digging around.

He pulled out a scrumpled up note and banged it onto the top of the fridge with his face all snarly and vicious.

Then he turned and walked out of the side door to the dining room and he was gone.

He didn't say hello.

When Mum saw me there she made a smile for me and said, 'I can go and get some shopping now. D'you want to come?'

When we were walking along the road she said, 'I hate having to ask all the time.' She looked really sad and tired. I don't know what I'm supposed to do. I don't say anything.

She made another smile for me and we walked to the corner shop and bought nice things.

Today we have cottage pie, and peas, and carrots, my favourite. Mum says to Tara and me that she's got a job in a bar so we can buy more things. She laughs and says, 'Ridiculous. I can't even afford light bulbs.'

If she's happy, everything's okay.

We don't see my dad for a while. He's fishing out of some other place for a bit.

It's nice. The house feels warm and the lights are all on.

Tara's in more. Her friends come round at night. Mine too. We listen to music and talk. I don't know what about. Just talk, and mess about.

Tara's friends start bringing drink round. Sometimes older boys come in and they're drunk already, being sick. She laughs and pushes them outside in the garden so they're not sick on the floor.

They play kissing games and strip poker so I go off to my room.

One night she calls me downstairs. This big boy I know a bit, Lance, is laying on the floor in our sitting room. He's not awake but he coughs. Every time he coughs, blood comes out on the rug.

Tara's kneeling on the floor next to him. She looks worried. 'Somebody's beaten him up on his way up here. He's drunk.'

I look at him laying on the floor; he looks big and red and heavy.

Her other friends are huddled about the room whispering. They look scared. Tara's the only one close, not afraid to touch him.

She looks up at me. 'You're the fastest, Alex. You have to run and get help.'

She tells me an address. 'Get Adrian. He'll know what to do.'

There isn't time to get dressed and I've only got shorts and a T-shirt on. I run outside and up the steps to the road. It's cold outside, very late, very dark, very silent. There are no cars.

I run along the main road, in and out of the orange street light glow, down a side road and up a smaller lane. I find the number on the house where Adrian lives. I ring the bell and stand back.

I'm a bit out of breath; I think that Lance may die and I might not have run fast enough to save him.

The door opens and light comes out into the lane. A man is there. I don't know him and he stares at me. He looks puzzled, but I say, 'Is Adrian in please?' I don't have time to say who I am, I just stand there breathing hard.

He looks at me again, mutters something. Other people come into the hallway, look out at me. I don't know why this is taking so long.

A tall boy with short hair comes to the doorway. I've never seen him before.

He's not smiling. 'What is it?'

Now I have to explain. I can see by his face that he wants to know, and he won't budge unless it's a good story. I can also tell he will fix it.

I tell him quickly. He stands quiet, thoughtful, steady. He doesn't move. He just listens.

He looks annoyed. He doesn't answer right off, just stares at me. He's thinking. Maybe he's thinking whether he should believe me or not.

Then he says, 'Okay. I'll come.'

I tell him the way, then I turn and run. I can't wait for him. He'll slow me down.

I race off. I run so fast that I overtip myself. I feel my head going forward. I go down with a smack and scrape along the tarmac so hard and so fast that it feels like I've ripped the skin off my knees and my shins, and the palms of my hands are burning and gritty.

I get up and run on but my legs feel stiff. When I get in Tara's still kneeling beside the big boy on the floor. I'm scared to go too close; I wonder if he's dead yet.

Adrian comes in soon after me. He speaks to Tara quietly. He bends down and talks to Lance on the floor though he doesn't get much answer, just blubbering lips but no noise, more coughing and blood. No movement. He's not dead; he's unconscious though.

Adrian goes into our dining room and I watch him pick up the phone. He asks for a number and writes it down. He makes another call, very short, says our address and gives directions.

When he comes in he says the boy's dad is coming to fetch him.

Tara's eyes look huge. 'No,' she says. 'But is he going to be okay? What about a doctor?'

I don't like it either, but I don't know why.

Adrian looks at me, and back to Tara. 'His dad says he's coming. I can't go against that.'

It seems ages.

A horrible, ugly, hairy old man arrives, smelly and scruffy. I don't like him.

He ignores all of us in the room. It's not our fault.

He walks across our carpet with his stinky boots. He gets hold of Lance under the armpits and Adrian steps forward to pick up his legs. I hold open the doors. They carry him up the steps to the road, and I follow. I want there to be an ambulance up there.

When we get to the road there's a battered old van parked up outside with the back doors open. It stinks of fish and there's hooks and nets inside and stinky dirty boxes.

Lance's dad throws the boy's body onto the grey metal floor of the van but his feet are still dangling down. His dad kicks them inside, makes a grunty noise when he does it, and slams the doors shut. He gets in the front seat and drives away.

He doesn't speak to us.

Adrian and I go back inside to tell Tara.

34

'What the hell happened to your knees?' she says. 'Don't tell Mum.'

As if.

One night Tara was having a party. I got bored and went upstairs to my room. I wasn't tired so I played with my hamster for a bit. I had to go outside with a bag of smelly sawdust and, just as I lifted the lid off the bin, I heard that black door to the road screech open and bang against the rail.

I spun round and looked up at my mum on the steps.

She was back from work.

'What the hell are you doing out here?!'

I stared at her. I guessed it must have got really late. 'I was just cleaning out my hamster cage.' It sounds a bit lame. I knew I wasn't doing anything wrong but I knew it wasn't quite right either.

She began to stomp down the steps. The lights were all on. The music was up loud.

I turned and ran in the door to warn the others. Tara's friends threw open the windows of the sitting room, jumped out and ran into the dark of the garden, down to the railway line and away.

My mum stormed into the house. Tara stood in the bright, noisy room looking innocent with huge eyes. I fled upstairs.

Tara's friends don't come round anymore. She goes out instead.

## 9

There's never anyone home now. I can't go upstairs to bed because it's too dark and I'm scared of the stairs. I'm scared of the hall too. It's lined with nearly black wood panels and the lights are off.

Even if I get myself out into the dark hall, past the black opening to the sheds, and as far as the bottom of the stairs, I still have to go up the dark stairs.

The stairs are dark and creepy. All up the stairs is lined with the same nearly black wood on both sides so, even if the light is on, it's still dark. When I first moved here I wouldn't go up late at night unless Mum stood at the bottom to see I made it to the top okay.

I used to creep up, not sure what would be round the bend. She thought I was silly. She stood so still and so silent I used to think she'd gone away. I used to say, 'You are still there, aren't you?' and she would sound cross and say,

'Of course I am. There's nothing to be afraid of. This is a nice house. There aren't any ghosts here.'

But there is something here, it's in the air.

One night I'm nearly at the top, almost round that dark bend. Suddenly everything goes black. I scream and crouch low.

Then I hear her giggling. 'Sorry,' she tries to say but she's laughing. 'I switched the light off. Sorry. I was only having a joke.'

I start to cry. I'm ashamed of it but I can't help it. I know I'm a coward about that kind of stuff. She switches the light back on and comes up to say sorry like she means it but she's still snuffling in her nose like she's trying not to laugh. I shove her away and run to my room.

I love football. It's ace, but our PE teacher, Mr Knowles, drives me nuts. He's got no idea. He knows I'm fast and he still won't let me play centre-forward.

He sticks me on defence every time we play, right-back every time. He doesn't give me a chance to score. I know I can do it.

I scuff about in the dirt at the empty end of the pitch. It's worse for the goalie.

I concentrate for a while, watching the ball, watching the tackles. And then I get bored.

I watch for ages and I'm getting cold keeping in my little square. It's all I'm allowed. If I get excited and run out of it and join in the game, Knowley shouts at me,

'Get back in there! Stay in position!'

I don't think he likes me.

I'm really cold, and really bored, thinking about other stuff. Next thing, the whole lot of them are on top of me, two teams it feels like, all in my little corner, smacking into each other and shouting,

'Here! Here!'

'Get off!'

'Pass it, Cox!'

I have to wake up quick and try to get rid of them.

Knowley gives me a look before he jogs after them, 'Dozey,' he says.

If I was a PE teacher I wouldn't be so stupid.


When there's a big storm in the winter, I go down to the beach at night. There's this huge wall built as a sea defence against the storms. If it wasn't there our town would be washed away by now. It's really clever.

It's very high, and built in a bendy shape so you can stand underneath it and it curves over, above your head. If you're on the top, it's a walkway. You can walk miles along it, and the trains rush past right beside you. It's really old but it's still strong and the sea never breaks through the wall.

I stand underneath in the storms. The massive waves crash down on the top of it, right across the railway line and sometimes they spray salt on our windows. I have to press close to the wall so they don't land on me and suck me out to sea.

It's all in the timing. I stand out in the open and watch the big waves. Then, when I can see a massive one building, I step back near the wall, wait while it rears up above me, and duck under the curve of the wall just as it smashes down. It makes a terrible crash when it falls.

The wind is shrieking so it makes me deaf for a bit. All the water swirls around my feet, and it roars and gurgles before it drains away. It's brilliant.

Scally never comes down there when I do that. I like to dare myself. I don't tell anyone because they'd tell me not to.

I never get caught. I don't even get my feet wet. Well, not much.


I wish someone was home. The nights in the winter time are really long. I lie on the floor in front of our gas fire in the dining room. I lie on the mat with Scally. He's warm. It's nice.

When Mum comes in I say I went to sleep, and try to look a bit surprised. I don't say I'm too scared to go upstairs into the empty dark.


My mum gets ready for Parents' Evening at my school. I'm in Year 8 now.

She looks colourful when she goes to work and she says the men look down her cleavage. She says they're harmless. 'It's fun working in a bar,' she says. 'It's a laugh.'

Tonight, she has to take the night off work but she still dresses up.

She comes downstairs looking smart, really different, not like a barmaid or my mum. I know when she walks into the hall at my school, people will turn and look. Her hair's just right, make up nice, and she's wearing a blue dress that makes her look like she's in charge. I wish I could go too, and see my teachers see her. I think my mum's the best looking mum in the school.

We had an Open Day when I was about seven, in primary. I had to wait by the school gate for her to come. The other mums had all gone in already. I waited in the sun.

It was very quiet. I heard clicking heels on the pavement and, round the corner she came. My stomach did a funny, twisty thing, she looked so good. And she was mine.
I went red I was so pleased. I thought my mum was the prettiest out of all the mums. She had on a navy blue dress, very smart, and navy shoes and a navy bag too. But her shoes were red, and her nails. I thought she looked like she should be the Queen.

Well, I was only seven.

I caught hold of her hand and led her through the gate, careful that she mustn't get dirty on anything. I led her along the corridors to my classroom. I introduced her to my friends and my teachers all the way, very smug. 'This is my mum.' She looked at all my work for the whole year. She said it was really good.

I have to wait until she comes home to hear what the teachers say about me tonight, but I know already.

She smiles and is kind but I think she's disappointed. I was top all the way through Year 7 and now I'm half way down the class. I can't help it. I can't concentrate.

## 10

My dad's home for roast on Sundays sometimes. Tara stays upstairs in her room till she has to come down. I always have to call her while Mum puts everything on the table.

My dad piles up his plate till it nearly overflows. He concentrates when he eats. He doesn't talk. When he clamps his teeth together, a big vein stands out on his forehead, and a grinding sound comes from somewhere inside his head. I always notice it but I try not to look at him. It's safer. When he stops being so hungry he looks up. He's staring at me.

'God! Look at him, doesn't eat enough to keep a bird alive!'

I shuffle about a bit in my chair but I don't look at him.

'What's the matter with you?' he says. 'D'you live on air? What are you cutting that meat all about for? That's not fat. You should be a surgeon.'

I try to smile because I know he means this as a joke even though I don't think it's funny. He says it every time. I don't like eating when he's staring at me anyway. I feel hot and stupid, but I feel really mad too.

I look at my mum and she's gone quiet.

Now he swings round on Tara. He's got a nasty look on his face.

'What's the matter with you? What are you staring into your food for? God! Look at the state of you, Spotty. Don't you ever wash?'

Tara doesn't say anything. She keeps her eyes down. She's gone really white.

We're all quiet, like we're not breathing.

'I'm out all weathers, earning the money to put food in your mouths.' He jabs his fork at me. 'He's picking away at it like it's not good enough, and she's as miserable as sin,' he says, and he jerks his chin at Tara. 'You kids don't know what hard work is.'

He jabs his fork at Tara now. 'You Madam, are going to have to get your finger out.'

I don't know what he means. He hates Tara. Even when she just sits quietly. He hates her all the time and she doesn't do anything.

My mum sounds tired, but a bit cross as well. 'Greg, please.'

Here it comes. He swings for Tara. 'What? What are you smirking at?' His hand catches her hard across the back of her head, even though she ducks. Down she goes. Her knife and fork crashes onto her plate. She's got tears in her eyes. She wriggles out from under his arm and the table and runs away up to her room.

My mum's angry now. I'm scared to death. I want to go up to Tara. I know she's crying up there on her own but I'm afraid to move because it'll draw attention to me. I don't like being such a coward.

Mum stands up, picks up Tara's plate and takes it upstairs. When she passes me it feels like she's on fire.

Tara eats most of her food on her own in her room. Some days she comes down to the town with me after. She never says anything about my dad. She talks about other fun things.

# 11

Our form tutor says we're the worst Year 8s they've had for years. I'm pretty pleased about this. I don't think we're bad. I think we're funny.

I have the best time ever at school. I love it. Something mad happens every day. Not horrid mad, funny mad. We get on great in my class and, most days, I laugh so much my guts hurt.

We've got this really quiet teacher for history. She's called Miss Beddow. She's quite old and has a sweet smile, smiling as if she's embarrassed. I think she likes us a lot but sometimes we go too far and she looks really worried when we won't pack it in.

We've been thinking how we can catch her out. It won't be hard because she doesn't see trouble coming. We come up with a really good plan.

Stacey brings in some pink wool from home. We have it ready at the back of the class, tied to my desk.

Liam calls Miss Beddow to the back, 'Miss, Miss. I don't understand.' It's some dumb question he's made up.

He has to work it so she has to come right back near the wall and peer at his book. I think he's overacting but she doesn't seem to notice. She looks pleased, like she really wants to help. She looks pink she's so pleased and, when I notice that, I feel a bit bad about what we're going to do.

While she's peering over Liam's desk I pass the ball of wool across to Jez. He winds it round the leg of his desk and passes it to Stacey. She does the same and passes it to me. I wind it round mine and pass it to Liam.

Miss Beddow is flagging, as if she senses that Liam's dumb questions are fake.

Jez sticks his hand up and gets her to turn sideways by his desk, 'Miss, Miss, can you look at my book? Is this right?'

We need her to stay still for a bit, and not move her legs.

We have to work fast, passing and looping the wool backwards and forwards, criss-crossing on itself. We're very quick and we get a brilliant cat's cradle set up between the four desks with Miss Beddow's legs in the middle of it.

Liam and Jez can't keep her there anymore.

She straightens up and says, 'Well now. We must get on.' She looks a bit tired with all the daft questions.

I'm impressed that she's kept her patience though. Almost any one of the other teachers would've whacked them both over the head with a heavy text book ages ago.

'Ooh! Ooh!' She yelps. Her eyes look huge.

'Ooh! Ooh! I'm trapped.' She's staring down at the pink net we've woven round her legs. She totally panics.

She tries to jump up and down, to get her legs out, but there's no place big enough to get her foot through.

We're all laughing 'cos we think she'll get the joke. But she has tears in her eyes and she's still hopping and going, 'Ooh! Ooh!' with big eyes. 'Get me out! Get me out!'

This isn't the result we wanted. I don't know what we wanted. I didn't imagine her getting teary. I feel bad.

We're laughing one second, then trying to get her free as fast as we can before she flips out. I'm pretty worried. She's in a right state.

She runs out of the classroom, crying, and we never see her again.

The Deputy Head, Mr Anderson, comes to take our next History class.

'You are extremely cruel children,' he says. 'I am mortified by your heartlessness.'

He tells us Miss Beddow won't be back to teach us anymore. He says she's had a nervous breakdown. I don't know what it is but it doesn't sound like a good thing.

It was only wool.

Tonight I get myself upstairs before it gets too dark. I have a bath to make the time go, and I stay in the warm in the bathroom. When I have to come out I can't. The bathroom door is at the top of the dark stairs. If I open the door there's all blackness out there. The empty box room is next door. Worst of all is the big black hole of the staircase, bending down into the black hallway and the dark sheds. I lock the door and stay in the bathroom. It's tiny in here, and the light is nice.

After a while I get really cold. I get a towel off the rail. Then I lie on the little mat on the floor and go to sleep.

I hear the front door open. My mum comes upstairs and taps on the door, 'Are you in there, Alex?'

I can come out now. 'I went to sleep,' I say.

'You funny thing,' she says. 'Why didn't you go to bed? You must be frozen.'

'I was warm enough. I had a towel.' I'm lying again.

## 12

It's Summer term. Old Knowley sets up hurdles for us to try. It's brilliant. I'm made for this. Now he can see how good I am.

We practice how to stretch out our leading leg and, at the same time, bend our other knee so our following leg is tucked up tight into the body. We do a few runs to get the feel of it before we jump our first hurdle. It's easy.

We set up the hurdles on the track, all spaced out the same distance apart. He gets us into groups of four and we line up ready to go. It's only 100 metres so I'm thinking sprint and knee, sprint and knee, as I belt off down the track. I catch one of the hurdles with the toe of my trainer. It goes down with a big bang but I can't stop to right it. It bugs me that I clipped one.

When we've all had a go, Knowley gets out his stopwatch and we do a few heats. We're down to the quickest four – David, Jez, Liam and me. I know I'm going to have them.

I'm focussed on the finish line, ears waiting for Knowley's whistle.

He blows. We're off. I belt down the track again. It's like my feet don't even touch the ground. I'm light, I'm fast, and I fly over those hurdles as if they're not even there.

Beside me, David thunders along. He's really going for it, hard and heavy. I hear bang, bang, bang, as he flattens the hurdles, just like he's stepping on the damn things.

I can't believe it. He passes me just as we get to the line.

Dan's off PE because of a cold or something. He brings his arm down as we run across the 100 metre line.

David is panting and he bends over like he's got stomach ache.

'Well done, David,' says Knowley, walking up. 'Very fast. Fourteen seconds.'

He turns to me, 'Second place, Alex Marshall.'

'Eh?' I say. 'He knocked down half the hurdles.'

Knowley ignores me. 'Third place Jez Farley, fourth place Liam Cox. Well done all of you.'

No fair. What's the point of having hurdles on the track if you flatten them instead of clearing them? I think Knowley's even more of a prat than I did before.


My dad's trying to get his boat in. There's a Summer gale. Mum says he's in trouble. I can't imagine my dad in trouble.

She heard about it on the radio. She says the Coastguard's sent out a helicopter to lift off his crew. We just have to wait for news now.

He doesn't come home. He phones Mum to say he won't be back tonight.

When he comes home he says his boat bottomed, three times. I'm by the door, listening. I imagine the *Pearl* rolling and pitching, water swilling round the decks, swamping her.

He laughs a hard sort of laugh, not a happy one. I hear him say, 'I got to the point where I'd rolled up my charts.'

I can't believe he'd do that. I can't believe he'd give up on the *Pearl*. I can't believe he'd give up, take his charts from the deckhouse, and be lifted off like his crew.

He didn't.

He brought the *Pearl* in single handed.

I go into the kitchen and ask him what it was like.

'Interesting,' he says. He rubs his scratchy old hands over his face. 'It was interesting.'

He's gone again by the time the 6 o' clock news comes on, and there he is, on our television. It looks weird to see him there, all unshaven and gruff.

I look at him. I don't know who he is really.

The interviewer sticks a microphone in his face and asks him what happened. He says, 'I understand the fish shifted in the hold, Mr Marshall?'

My dad says, 'That's right.'

'And is it true that the *Pearl*'s hull grounded three times while you were trying to bring her in.'

'That's right.'

'Your crew had been lifted off. Why didn't you leave the boat with them?'

'I had fish to land.'

'Oh.' The interviewer laughs. 'And did you get into the fish market in time?'

'No.' My dad grins then. 'It was a bad day for us.'

That was it. 'A bad day for us.' I stare at the screen. He's gone. He doesn't tell a very good story. His crew airlifted off in the teeth of a gale, tons of fish all sloshed over onto one side of the *Pearl*, his boat bouncing off the seabed. I think this is a good story but I have to imagine it for myself.

I can't throw a javelin quite right. I reckon it would work better if I was a bit taller. The javelin's pretty heavy and it's way taller than me. Knowley's really patient. He shows us loads of times how to hold it and how to make the run up.

I do the run up okay but I stop when I try to throw it. I know it's meant to be all one motion but, because I stop, it doesn't fly very far. I'm really disappointed. I keep trying though. It's got to get smoother.

Knowley's got a thing about us all walking slowly off to one side and back behind the line after we've collected our javelin. The next person's not allowed to run up and throw until the field is clear.

We get this whole choreographed thing going. Run up and throw – or stall and throw if it's me – jog forward, retrieve the javelin, walk to one side and return. Next person runs up, throws and on we go. We're all doing this and we look pretty well drilled. I'm getting better at it too.

Next time we have a go, a week after, Knowley's not there. He's off watching some of the other kids long-jumping into the sand pit.

Next thing, here he is, running over, purple in the face like he's going to go bang, and splatter all of us with Knowley bits.

'You b****y idiots! What the hell do you think you're doing?!'

I wasn't watching, but Knowley's seen James throw his javelin before Liam has walked clear and got back behind the line. He's going ape. I'm glad it wasn't me.

After a bit, he stops shouting. He must see that we don't get it and he quiets right down. He tells us that, when he was a teenager, a kid threw the javelin and it went clean through another kid's back. Right through his back and out the front of his chest. He looks white now, a bit ill. I feel a bit ill too.

I imagine it every time I throw the javelin after that, imagine the sharp silvery metal ramming into some kid's back with a great bang, bursting out through the ribs, bits of bone and blood everywhere. It makes me feel sick.


I haven't seen Ryan for ages. We went round to visit Auntie Sarah and he was there. He was back from the young offenders place for a day out. His hair's all short. He looks like an ant.

He doesn't say much. He doesn't even really look at me. He talks to Tara, but he looks really quiet, like he's not funny anymore.

When we get home Tara's pretty quiet too. She says Ryan told her something and I'm not to tell. She says Ryan was helping our dad with the boats on the beach front last summer. He headed off home but he forgot his jacket. When he went back down the beach to get it from the hut the door wasn't padlocked. He pushed it open. My dad was in there, with some girl, and they were doing it.

I really don't want to imagine this. It's pretty sick.

Ryan said my dad jumped up, chased him, and beat the crap out of him, said he'd kill him if he ever told. Ryan didn't tell anyone. He's told Tara now though. Tara says I have to keep it secret. Mum mustn't know. Nobody knows but us three. I love Ryan. I hate my dad for hurting Ryan.

13

A new history teacher's come to take over because Miss Beddow's gone mad. He's called Mr Wellman but he doesn't look that well. He's a funny colour. He's got a very quiet voice, and he moves slowly, like he feels definite about things. He wears old clothes. We don't think he ever washes them - a brown tweed sports jacket, with leather patches on the elbows, grey trousers, old brown shoes.

We pretend we want to know things, like we did with Miss Beddow. He likes it too.

'Sir! Sir! Can you help me with this?'

He comes to our desks, and he looks really disappointed because we're messing him about. He's just target practice.

We flick ink at the back of his jacket.

He walks past the front rows and the kids at the front have a shot at it. When he stops to listen to whoever's stuck his hand up, he cocks his head on one side, and leans slightly forward. Then the kids at the back and the side of him can have a go.

The blue patch on his back gets bigger and darker. By Christmas it's nearly eight inches long, shaped like a diamond, so dark it's almost black. This is brilliant teamwork, stealth, timing and accuracy. We are hunters.

We do it every Thursday afternoon. I don't know why. We just do. It seems strange that he doesn't notice when he gets home. It looks really funny when he walks down the corridor ahead of us.

When we come back to school in January it's still there. Awesome. We carry on flicking, harder.

On Tuesday morning, the Deputy Head, Mr Anderson, strides into our form room. He's tall and he's got no sense of humour. He stands there and just stares at us. Really hard. We shut up. He stands there, staring. I feel really ashamed. He doesn't have to tell us what he's come in for. He lets us sweat for a bit.

Then he says really mean things to us. His voice sort of booms out.

53

'You are <u>all</u> going to be punished. You are unkind and irresponsible. Have you no kindness or sensitivity at all, none of you? I am disgusted by your behaviour.'

The way he says 'disgusted' makes it sound like he phlegmed it up.

The whole class gets detention after school, we have to club together and pay for the dry-cleaning bill, and we all have to write a letter of apology. Every single one of us. It makes me feel better when I've written mine though.

Mr Wellman comes into class the next Thursday afternoon and he doesn't say a word about it. He starts the lesson quietly and definitely, just like always. And his jacket's all clean.


My dad looks round the door of my room at night. He stares in, looks at me and goes away again. He's all narrow eyed, watchful, prowly. I hear him go back downstairs. He paces about in the kitchen. He's like a big cat in a zoo.

Mum's not allowed to work in a bar any more. My dad thinks the men look at her too much. She's got a job in a hospital now.

She wears a mauvy colour nurse's uniform and her hair's all scraped back. Old ladies die in the hospital and she holds their hands till they go. She cries about it sometimes when she gets home. 'They haven't got anyone,' she says. 'It's not right.' But she still likes it there.

Sometimes, funny and rude things happen to the patients and she tells Tara and me. She says she's not supposed to tell, so we don't tell anyone at school or anything. I don't want to go to hospital and have nurses like my mum laughing at my bare bum and stuff. She's really bad like that.

I'm half way down the stairs when my mum comes out of the kitchen. She looks wild. There's a huge crash from the kitchen.

She grabs me and drags me back up the stairs. She pulls me along the hallway. Another crash. 'He's gone berserk,' she says, with her eyes so big they've taken over her whole face.

I never saw her look like that. But 'berserk?' What kind of word's that? She's frightened and I'm frightened, but her big eyes and the stupid sounding word make me want to laugh at the same time.

She nearly falls over trying to get us down the narrow passageway. I'm thinking that the worst place to be is up here. I don't know why she didn't get straight outside. Instead she drags me into Tara's room and slams the door. Tara's out.

She's got hold of me like she's going to crush me to death. She's sort of covering me up. It's seriously weird. The noise downstairs is really bad. Smashing glass and falling and breaking things, throwing things, banging and him shouting.

My dad is yelling down there all by himself.

I don't know what's going on. 'What's he saying?'

She doesn't answer me. She's staring at the door, her eyes still big.

Tara's window is small and high up. It's in the gable end of the house. There's no way out of here. There's a tiny cupboard built into the wall of Tara's room but my dad knows it's there so it's no use us getting in that, even if we could fit. We can't climb out of the window because we'll break all our bones if we jump.

We're both scrunched up on the floor. She's got hold of me so tight I can hardly breathe. We don't move, we don't talk, but we stare at the door.

After a while the noise isn't so loud downstairs, smaller bangs and smashes, not so much yelling. We stay in Tara's room. It's getting late.

We can't hear anything.

Mum gets up and says she'll go down. I follow her.

He's gone. Everything is broken.

# 14

I haven't seen my dad for a bit. I found a rusty old fishing knife on the tide line so I keep it under my pillow just in case. I never know when he's going to be back, and I have to keep watch.

When Tommy comes round for me, he has to come upstairs and wake me up most mornings. I can't wake up, I'm tired. I have to get dressed really quick and run for the bus. Tommy gets annoyed because we miss it sometimes and then we're in trouble at school.

When I get in from school today, Mum says she wants to talk to me. She's sitting at the table in the dining room with a cup of tea, like she's been waiting. It feels silly sitting down at the table with my mum to talk. She looks all sensible. It's like talking to a teacher.

She says Dad's gone away for a while, to a hospital. She says he's got an Obsession. I thought he was away fishing somewhere.

She says he's got an Obsession and he has to have some treatment. The doctors say he has to have ECT. I don't know what this is but I can't imagine my dad having anything done to him. He's going to though.

She tells me it means they're going to stick things on his head and electrocute his brain to try and break the Obsession. I think this sounds horrible. I even feel a bit sorry for him.

She says the doctors told her it might work, but it might make him more violent. Mum looks pretty grim when she says that.

She goes to visit him sometimes. I don't.

When he comes home he's a bit quieter. He doesn't move so quick and he looks safer. He made a coffee table while he was in the hospital. I look at it and think it can't have anything to do with him. I can't imagine him making things. I can't imagine anyone telling him what to do, unless they tied him up first.

He doesn't say much. He looks a bit more like a pet than a wild thing now, but he goes to the kitchen cupboard a lot. He's got some bottles of pills high up in the top one, and he rattles tablets in his pocket like he needs to know they're there.

There's a youth club set up in the town. It's in an old warehouse near the quay. Some of the Year 11s have organised it. We go down there every week, on Fridays. I quite like it. I don't dance though. Stacey does. And Louise, and Ally. Girls like that stuff.

There are wooden steps going up into a little box where one guy, Martin Tapper, plays the music. I go up there and talk to him sometimes. He lets me choose what music I like and he puts it on. The walls are painted black and he's got a machine that sends coloured lights in patterns over the walls. Stacey looks really pretty dancing in the coloured lights. She smiles up at me and makes a face to say, 'Come on,' but I won't. No way.

Tommy's parents have gone away for the weekend. I'm going to stay over at his house. We think it will be fun to get drunk and go to the youth club. We have to find someone to buy us some drink though. I'd ask Tara but I never see her. We hang about outside our supermarket and see if anyone we know comes by.

It's ages. This guy, Paddy, comes along and we ask him. He doesn't look like he wants to. I have to talk him round for hours before he gives in. I tell him to get us a bottle of wine each and give him the money. He goes in. We try to look casual till he comes back, in case anyone's watching.

Paddy doesn't look very happy when he comes out, but he gives us the wine.

'You will be careful?' he says.

I put the bottles in my backpack. 'We'll be fine. It'll be a laugh.'

We go down to the quay, get the bottles open, and get it down as fast as we can.

The wine is sticky and sweet, really gross. I get the first half of it down okay but I have to force the last bit. We chuck the bottles in the sea and, when I throw mine, I feel horrible, like my head weighs a ton and it's pulling me over.

I laugh and think, this is drunk then. That was quick.

Tommy's giggling and bumping into a pile of crab pots and coiled ropes. I feel ill. It's like I'm going round and round, everything spinning round me at the same time. It's sort of funny but sort of nasty.

We stumble off to the youth club, but we try to walk straight because we think people are staring at us. Dave Rice is on the door. I like Dave. He plays football for our school. He's the best scorer. He's always nice to me when I see him up on the games field.

He won't let us in at first. He says, 'Have you been drinking?'

I grin at him like an idiot. 'Just some wine.' I'm feeling pleased with myself.

He scowls at me. 'How much?'

'A bottle.' My legs are bending around underneath me.

'You've had a bottle, just the two of you?' He sounds shocked.

I think he's silly. 'No.' I wave my arm as if that's nothing. 'We had one each.'

'One each?!' He's staring at us now as if we're mad. Then he grabs me.

He catches hold of both my arms, yanks me into the corner and sits me down hard on a table. I don't mind. He talks to some of the others, Martin and a big girl. I sit there and watch everyone coming and going, Stacey, Louise, Jez, Liam, everyone. People stare at me but I can't hear what they're saying.

Dave looks at me sometimes, a bit frowny, when he's not seeing to other things. I smile at him. I don't seem to be able to do anything else, but that's okay.

I hear him whispering, and someone says that Tommy's outside throwing up in the drain. Poor Tommy.

It must be ten. Everybody's going home. I'm slumped in the corner when they go past.

People are moving about, coats and bags and things, bumping me. Dave pulls me off the table and half carries me outside. My legs aren't working at all. I can hear voices. He pushes me into the back of a little car. Tommy's already in there. He looks asleep. There's a big girl in the driving seat. She's talking to Dave through the window.

He reaches his hand in and shakes me. 'Alex, Alex. Wake up.'

'Whazzamadder?'

'Where d'you live? Hannah's going to take you home.'

'Going Tommy'zouse.'

More voices. Car door opens and shuts. Footsteps. Voices. Talking, talking all the time. Why don't they shush?

The car's moving. Maybe I'm asleep now. It bumps around then stops. The big girl opens the door. She tries to pull Tommy and me out of the car. We get out and fall in the road.

'Are you guys gonna be okay?'

I wave my arm up at her and smile. 'Yeah. Thankzfuh thlift. Verr nice.' I don't know how she found his house. Tommy gets in the doorway and I crawl in after him.

I can hear Tommy throwing up again but I go to sleep on the floor in his sitting room. It's too difficult to go upstairs.

I wake up in the middle of the night with a horrible lurchy feeling in my stomach. I make it up the stairs to the bathroom, only just. I hurl my guts up into his toilet and the smell of wee near the rim makes me throw up even more. I throw up so hard that my forehead hits the white china and bounces off. The vomit stinks, foul wine and sour smelly. I throw up again. I throw up so hard it's like my guts are right up in my throat.

After a bit I fall onto the floor by the toilet. There's sick on the carpet but I can't clean it up now. I want to go to sleep but I can't shut my eyes. It's too dangerous. If I keep them open the room will stay still. When I close them the room whirls round, faster and faster until I throw up again.

The lurchy feeling comes back. I'm so tired. I keep hurling, my head in the toilet, hurling and hurling, nasty little dribbles of green-yellow slime.

Tommy sticks his head round the bathroom door. I can't see him but I know he's there.

'You all right, mate?'

I try and lift my head up off the carpet but it's too heavy. I can see him though. He's standing up. I don't know how he does that. I can't move. I feel too ill.

I'm going to die. I wish it would happen quick so I don't have to feel like this anymore.

'I'll get some water.'

And he's gone.

When he comes back, I'm still hurling. Nothing really comes out, just a vile stinky sour smell and a belchy noise. It's a really ugly way to die but I don't care. I just want it over.

Tommy puts a glass of water near me. 'You look awful.'

I can't answer.

'I'm okay.' He sounds really happy. 'I was sick last night instead.'

He bends down and looks at me. 'I think I chucked it all up before it went through me.' He looks at me again. 'I'm going to get some breakfast. Want any?'

I retch again.

I hear him going away, downstairs.

I can hear the TV. I pull myself up. It's bright sunshine outside. I go downstairs one step at a time, on my bum. Tommy's got the footie on. It must be afternoon.

61

'You all right now?' He looks pleased to see me.

I lie on the rug in front of the TV and go back to sleep.

I stay at Tommy's till just before his parents come home on Sunday night. I can't go home like this in the day. My mum'll see me.

He calls for me, like always, on Monday morning. He always looks happy in the morning. Tommy's ace.

At break time I come round the corner of the long corridor near my classroom and Dave's there. I see him, then he sees me, then I turn back and go the other way. I can't go past him. I'm too embarrassed.

This isn't what I want to do. I want to say thanks to him for being so nice to me on Friday. I want to say I'm sorry I'm such an idiot. But I daren't. He's too good. I don't deserve to know nice people. I just hide from him.

# 15

I've just been in town with Jez and Tommy. We sit on the wall by the amusement arcade. Liam and Dan come by sometimes. We hang around. It's sort of our place.

Jez and Tommy head off for tea so I walk home.

I open the front door and walk smack into my dad. He's come down the stairs so he's all wrapped up in the dark and I can't see him too clearly.

My eyes adjust after a bit and he looks different. All soft somehow.

He's got a bag.

He's looking at me all funny. And he whispers.

He's got a scratchy loud voice usually. It kind of hurts your ears like you've just heard a gun go off or something. Loud and nasty. It makes me jump.

Today, though, he whispers. I don't get it.

He catches hold of me. I pull away. I'm nervous of his hands, but he catches hold gently. I don't understand this either.

He's looking all soggy and sad. 'Your mum wants me to leave.' He's looking right into my eyes as he says it, and I feel responsible somehow. I know that sounds funny, but I do.

His eyes are pouring something into mine. I wish he wouldn't look at me like this. I don't like it.

He hugs me.

It feels nice. Warm.

He's strong and soft, and I like the hug.

'Do you want me to go?' he says, all whispery.

I don't know. I really don't. He looks so lonely and sad that I don't think I can tell him to go away.

'No,' I say. Although I feel a bit muddled when I say it.

He pulls back a bit and looks into my eyes again. 'You love me, don't you?'

I have to think about this. No-one's ever asked me this before. I've never thought about love. He's just my dad.

I feel something. I'm not sure what it is. I know he can be quite nice sometimes. I remember.

I remember him laughing when I was quite little. He smiled sometimes, laughed sometimes. He looked nice when he smiled.

He came and got me out of bed one night, when I was so small I don't think I could even talk yet. 'The Royal's on fire,' he said. He lifted me up, dumped me on his shoulders, still in my pyjamas, and walked off into the town in the dark. He was striding along fast. We came round a corner and he pointed.

Mum was holding Tara's hand. Tara shrieked so Mum picked her up. Huge flames were roaring out of every window of a huge building. They were so big they curled up and over the roof. Lots of people were watching. Big yellow and red flames, crackling and spitting up into the dark sky.

And I remember him singing and playing a guitar. I must have been about four then. I don't know if he was any good at it. He looked happy doing that.

One day he came home to get me. I was playing in the garden.

He was grinning. 'There's a basking shark washed up on the beach. Come on.'

He walked so fast my legs couldn't keep up. I had to nearly run to keep close behind. When we got to the back beach he shook his head. 'Look at the size of that.'

A big, smelly, bluey black thing was slumped on the sand. Lots of people were cutting big square chunks out of it. For their cats they said. Poor stinky fish.

My dad laughed at them for being so silly. 'Someone had better tow that back out to sea quick or we won't be able to breathe round here.'

I remember him trying to explain to me how a turbine engine worked, and being pleased when I got it. I was pleased too. I like engines. They make sense.

I remember all this about him and I say, 'Yes.'

'You do love me?' he says.

I don't sound so certain. 'Yes.'

I feel like something's just been taken from me. I don't know what.

I felt all warm and full when he was hugging me.

Now I feel empty.

He smiles. He looks really pleased.

He puts down his bag in the hall with a thump and shoves open the kitchen door. He goes in and closes it behind him and I hear him say something to Mum.

I don't feel very comfortable. I go up to my room.

A bit later my mum sticks her head round my door. Her face is all twisty and she spits words at me. 'He says you want him to stay?'

It's a question but it's something else as well. Her eyes are angry at me.

I know I've done the wrong thing. But I don't know how to take it back.

Now he's here nearly every day. Tara keeps well clear. She's got in with some new friends. She says she's tried smoking dope, that it's great.

I liked her other friends. They were noisy and got drunk a lot but they were really funny. Her new friends look wet. Boring and half asleep. No fun at all.

I know when he's here because I come down to the kitchen in the morning and there's buckets on the floor with crabs inside. Some of them get out, even with a rubber band on their claws, out and rattling round on our floor. I think they might get hold of my toes.

Poor things, being caught by my dad.

65

He gets a long thin skewer and punctures them. Then he drops them in boiling water.

One morning I find lobsters in the sink. They're really big and blue.

My mum looks at my dad like he's crawled in from somewhere but she smiles when she eats the fresh scallops.

I can't see the point of having my dad at home. He's just there. He doesn't do anything except watch TV a lot. He's always asleep in the chair but, if I creep in and turn off the TV, he jolts awake and shouts, 'What are you doing? I was watching that.' He wasn't. If Tara comes in he yells mean things like, 'Look at the ass on you. You're getting fat.'

He prowls about, looking fierce, but he doesn't talk much. Mum looks at him like she hates his guts. She snipes at him. I don't like the way she says things. It makes him look small. He looks like some kind of wounded creature when she says mean stuff. I feel sorry for him then.

Sometimes I come in and he's sitting at the dining room table, holding his face. He's crying. It's horrible.

I keep out of the way, stay on the beach mostly.

I don't know why he's so vile to Tara. I know he doesn't like her but I don't know why.

He's home again today, slumped in a chair with the TV on, and she comes into the sitting room. I can see by her face that she didn't know he was in here. She steps in the door, looks at him, stops and steps back. Then she makes a little frown face, steps forward and keeps moving, quiet and determined.

I can see she's going to walk round behind the chair, as if maybe he won't see her if she's quick.

He's like a great animal somehow. He swings round so fast. He looks as if he's watching TV but it's like he senses her there, even though she doesn't make any sound when she comes in. I see her watching him as she moves by, really quiet.

'What the hell are you doing?' He snarls at her.

It's weird. He always snarls at her. He never snarls at me. He calls me 'the boy.' He says it like being the boy is a good thing, with a kind of warm sound in his voice. When he says 'her' and 'she' about Tara it sounds like he's got a mouth full of that sicky bile stuff I was chucking up into Tommy's toilet. He never says her name. Ever.

'Look at the state of you!'

Tara looks down at the carpet and keeps moving, smooth as a cat, but it doesn't work. It's like the more she tries to be invisible the more mad he gets.

'Dirty little bitch,' he snarls. 'You stink. I can smell you from here.'

Tara's face goes red. She doesn't look at him, or me. She picks up a top that she's come in for, gets out of there and goes back upstairs.

I look at him. He's smiling. Then he sees me looking.

'What are you staring at? That girl stinks.' He looks pleased with himself. He yells towards the open doorway. 'You need a shower, maid.'

I leave my homework on the table, get up and walk out. I don't want to be anywhere near him. He makes me sick.

# 16

Auntie Sarah's my dad's sister but I've got another aunt near London. She's my mum's sister. I don't see her that much but she sends me nice stuff sometimes. A book at Christmas, something on my birthday. This time she's sent me a new sweatshirt. It's really cool. It fits and everything. I don't know how she knows.

Last week a boy in my class had his Bar mitzvah. I didn't know he was Jewish. He never said. He's got this really cool stuff, loads of it, but the coolest thing is this amazing sound system his parents got him. It must have cost loads. Awesome.

I asked him why he got so much stuff. 'I had a big party,' he said. Loads of his family came and brought him presents. He says that's what always happens at Bar mitzvah.

He says his whole family come round every Friday night and they have a big dinner and talk a lot. So that's what he's doing when the rest of us are down at the youth club in the dark, with the coloured lights on the wall. I wonder if other families do that.

My dad's back at sea now. It's okay at home.

I've been out kicking a ball round all afternoon with Tommy, down at the park. I'm coming along the main road back towards my house and I see a taxi driving away. We don't know anyone who would come and see us in a taxi. It's a long way. When I get there, the black gate's banging open against the rail.

I pull it shut and go down the steps. There's no sign of anyone but I hear a big crash from inside. I push open the front door. It takes a second for my eyes to adjust to the dark in the hallway.

My mum's standing at the bottom of the stairs with her face all stretched and weird, like she's moaning without any noise coming out.

She sees me and says, 'Oh no, Alex. You'd better not come in.'

Well, I'm in already.

There's a big groaning noise and I see a black heap on the floor at the bottom of the staircase. It starts to move, hauling itself up like a beast. It looks like my dad.

He's fumbling around trying to get his hand into the back pocket of his jeans but he can't do it. It's like he's crippled.

He's groaning and fumbling. I don't know what he wants out of his pocket. I go to help him but Mum says, 'No, Alex. Keep back.'

She looks like she wouldn't go near him, even with a big stick.

He gets himself up onto his knees and pulls himself up to nearly standing. He looks completely mad. His face is all purple and his hair is sort of lumpy, like somebody's mussed it. He's still groaning and trying to get a hand into his back pocket. He's saying something that sounds like 'money.' He must have lost some.

He goes down with a big bang. I've never seen a man fall down. He goes down so hard and so heavy I think he must make a massive hole in the floor. My mum looks wild, her eyes all starey. 'Get me a pillow, quick,' she says.

I run off to their room. They've got two beds pushed together. I grab a pillow from the nearest one.

When I get back with it he's up again. I give Mum the pillow and she darts about from side to side holding it out in front of her. When he goes down again she shoves the pillow out so his head hits it.

He's amazing. He still gets up again. He just won't stay there. He drags himself back up, holding onto the stair post and starts trying to get himself up the stairs. He's mad. He'll never make it.

My mum looks embarrassed, like she's ashamed, even though she hasn't done anything. 'He's drunk. I'm sorry you came home to this.'

My eyes feel all starey too. It's really scary seeing my dad dragging himself about like some kind of swamp monster from a horror film. I want it to stop. If he'd just lie down and go to sleep it would be okay, but he won't.

He gets half way up the stairs and he's even managed to get upright, on his feet.

I'm at the bottom watching and then he starts to turn, slowly swivelling, like a tree that's going to come down.

'Alex, get back!' Mum yells at me and I sidestep as he comes down, head first, down the stairs. He hadn't even made it to the bend. His body turns through nearly 180 with his feet still stuck on the stair, and she jumps in front of him with the pillow, rams it between his head and the wall. He lands hard on the floor, his neck all bent and his head jammed against the doorframe.

She made it with the pillow though. She's a quick mover.

He groans. 'Let me die. Why don't you let me die?'

Mum's sitting on the floor by him. It looks like she's trying to get his head on straight. She looks up at me sort of pleading and desperate. Then she looks a bit teachery again. 'Go and make some tea or something, Alex.'

I'm thinking, if he wants to die, why doesn't she let him. I would. He's not much use. I bring her the tea.

When he's sleeping she takes me up to the road. 'He keeps groaning about some money. Help me look. It might be up here.'

We look around on the grass verge. 'He should have had a roll of cash in his back pocket from the fish market,' she says. 'Three weeks pay. It's gone.'

There's no money anywhere up here. Mum pokes about in the grass. 'He keeps saying someone's stolen it.'

He probably just lost it in the pub. Stupid.

Mum says a taxi driver came down and rang the bell. She went to the door but he'd gone back up the steps. She went up to the road and he'd tipped my dad out onto the verge outside the house, where everyone could see the state he was in. I know she's thinking what the people across the road must have been thinking, but it's not her fault.

I didn't see her up there. I don't know how she got him down the steps and in the door.

She couldn't get him any further though. He's still asleep on the floor at the bottom of the stairs. I don't want to go near him.

I was out playing footie with Tommy today. I walk in and I can hear yelling.

I look into the sitting room and there's my mum beating her fists on my dad's back. She's screaming, 'Greg! Get off her! Get off her!'

My dad's punching Tara as hard as if she's a man.

I shout at them. 'What the hell are you doing?!'

It looks like he's half killed Tara. I can't see her very well. She's all crouched over, taking the blows. She's not crying though. The only one crying is my mum.

He hears me and slows down. It's like he couldn't hear anything when my mum was yelling. He was too busy. I suppose he was getting tired when I shouted.

Tara gets free from him, shoots off upstairs and slams her door. Mum stares at me, all red faced and teary. Dad flings a look at me. 'Get outta here!'

I run away as well, upstairs to Tara's room. She doesn't let me in at first but I won't go away until she does.

She's sitting on her bed, crying, but really angry. She says Mum read her diary, that she'd written something in there about taking cocaine. She says my mum called in the drug squad.

'She what?' Even I know this is a bad and weird thing for my mum to do. We both know she's a bit green, but how could she think that was smart?

'Mum says she wanted to give me a fright.' Tara blows her nose and flings away the tissue. 'While they were here, questioning

72

me, trying to find out where I got it, Dad came home and went crazy.'

She says Dad's threatening to put us both In Care. I don't know what this means but I don't like the sound of it. I ask her what for, and she stares at me.

'He says Mum can't bring us up properly, so we'll have to go.'

# 17

I don't see much of Tara. I don't mind too much. She flips out at
the slightest thing. She started having a go at me a few weeks ago.
She never used to do that, but she does it a lot these days. She
always used to look out for me.

I put up with it for a bit then I got sick of it. I answered her
back yesterday and she completely lost it. I gaped at her because
she looked like a wild thing, screaming at me.

When she came at me I thought she was going to hit me in
the face so I put my head down to avoid the punch. I wasn't
expecting it, but she came at me fast, grabbed hold both my
shoulders and brought her knee up hard into my face. I thought
she'd broken my nose.

It made me cry. It hurt like anything. It felt like my teeth
were smashed.

I put my hands up to feel my face, to see what was stove in
and she comes over. Sorry now. Crying. Wants to kiss and make
up. That's sick, that is.

I shoved her away and cleared off down to the beach with
Scally.

I hate it here.

My mum and dad are getting ready to go to the Police Ball. Mum
looks really special, like a film star. She comes into my room and
shows me. She's wearing sparkly ear-rings and a dress that
shimmers, with buts cut out of the sides so her waist is showing.
She's got a suntan.

She turns around and does a little dance for me. She's nuts.
She's a good dancer though. She tries to make me dance with her.
No way. When she was young, before she met my dad, she used to

dance in competitions. She's not allowed to anymore. My dad doesn't like her dancing with other people.

My dad looks a bit weird in a suit, like it's someone else's. He keeps tugging at his collar and tie like he's being choked. He looks nice though, tall, with black hair and brown eyes and really white teeth. He's like a Spanish pirate.

I'm asleep. I hear a funny, waily sort of noise that wakes me up. I can't make it out. It's all dark in my room but the waily noise gets loud, then it gets murmury. Then I hear my dad's voice all snarly and slurry. Then my mum's voice, 'Alex. Alex.'

I wake up properly when I hear that.

I get up and come out of my bedroom into the dark hallway. I can hear my mum's voice like she's begging. My dad sounds like he's growling. Then, there's a thud and my mum cries out like she's really hurt.

I creep down into the black of the stairs, round the bend with the triangle steps. I stay low, underneath the wooden side. There's no gaps in it so they can't see me.

My mum's crying.

I have to keep quiet.

I move really slowly so they don't hear me, and straighten up enough to look over the top of the stair sides.

I can see my dad sideways on with his arms held out in front of him. His face looks red-brown and all screwed up. He looks really ugly.

He's muttering something but I can't make out what it is. He gets louder, his arms jerk and there's another thud and my mum cries out again. He's bashed my mum's head against the block wall of the porch.

I look out further and he's got both his hands tight round my mum's throat and he's squeezing so his face gets redder. I can't see her too well.

I want to run up to him and get him off her but I can't. I really want to but I'm too scared. I daren't come out from behind the wooden side. I feel like such a coward. I can't come out. So I yell.

I yell at him so loud it's like my lungs burn. 'F*** off! You f***ing bastard!' My throat burns too.

He turns to look at me. He looks wild and mad and so angry that I nearly run upstairs. But I don't.

I have to stop him.

I think he's going to let go of her and come for me, but he doesn't.

He keeps at it. He's choking her, smacking her head against the block wall and shouting at the same time. Thud, thud, 'See what you've done. See how you've made the boy speak to me!'

I keep yelling. 'You f***ing bastard! You f***ing get off her!' I'm shocked at my own words. I never say stuff like this. I don't know where it comes from. It comes out by itself, but I have to keep at it till he stops.

My mum sounds weak. 'Please,' she says. 'Greg, please. Think of the children -,'

She's tired. Her voice is barely coming out. It sort of croaks and fades away.

I yell at him again. My throat's on fire. 'Get off her! Leave her alone you f***ing bastard!'

I feel such a coward. I'm a coward because I can't come out and cross that hall to where he's standing. My eyes are nearly popping out with yelling so hard.

He lets go.

He steps back, swaying slightly.

My mum's sobbing. She runs past him, past me, grabs hold of my arm and we bundle up the stairs.

I push her into my room and slam the door. She falls on the floor. Tommy stayed over the night before and I've got a mattress down there.

I say she should have my bed but she won't. She's still crying but really feeble and weedy, which she isn't. Not ever.

I cover her up with my quilt and she curls up like she can't get any smaller, all sniffly into the pillow.

I hear him at my door. I grab the handle. He tries to turn it. I hold it as tight as I can so he can't. If he turns the handle we've had it.

I grip it with all my strength and set up yelling again. 'You dare. You f****ing dare come in this room. You just f***ing dare!'

He tries the handle for ages and I'm thinking I can't hold it much longer. I'm still yelling, 'Bastard. F*** off!'

I feel him let go his side. I keep hold. I don't trust him.

'Don't speak to your father like that.' He shouts it but it's slurry and I can hear the tone is different. His voice sounds nasty but it doesn't have power in it. The words are tough, the sound is tough, but the energy's run out.

I'm staring at the closed door. It's like my stare has so much strength in it that my door will never open. I've willed it shut.

After a bit I hear him move and his bedroom door shuts. It's right opposite mine. He's less than a metre away.

I sit on my bed. I watch my mum. She's sleeping now but she's still sniffling as if she's not properly asleep.

I sit up and watch all night. I feel for the knife under my pillow. It's there. I sit on my bed watching the door. I don't sleep.

I must do though, because I wake up. My light's still on, Mum's still asleep on the floor, and it's daylight.

I go outside and he's gone. I didn't hear him go.

Mum looks awful when she wakes up. I bring her some tea and she sets off crying again, all stormy. She says my dad got mad because she danced with one of the policemen, and he thinks she fancied him. She swears she doesn't.

I don't care about that.

I wonder where my dad's gone. And when he'll be back.

Mum sends me to stay with my Granddad. It's her old dad and he lives in a flat. It smells funny.

He's really kind to me. He lets me sleep in his bed even though I don't want to. He's old. It's his bed. I say I can sleep on the sofa but he makes a fuss of me and gets the bed made up all clean and special.

We eat food out of tins, corned beef, and soup, beans on toast, stuff like that.

He's got an old reel to reel tape player that he got from a junk shop and he plays me music on it. We get on great.

Tara's gone to stay with a friend. I don't know where Mum is. I don't know where Scally is either.

## 18

Dan runs to get me at school in our lunch hour. He says Tara's up on the games field, by the old cricket pavilion and she wants me. It's broken and rotten wood, half fallen down, and it's out of bounds up there. The teachers think the kids will smoke behind the building if they're allowed up there. They do.

I run up to the field. I can't see her. I have to go round the back of the pavilion without anyone seeing or they'll report me for smoking. I don't smoke so that wouldn't be fair.

Tara hears me and comes out by the side, in the overgrown bushes.

'Hi Alex.' She looks a bit mucky, like she hasn't washed. She used to look really pretty. She's smiling though, so she still looks nice.

I look round behind me. I'm sure someone'll see me up here. 'I can't stay here. What've you come for?'

She smiles again. Like the old Tara. She looks naughty. 'I was in London.'

I stare at her. I thought she'd gone to stay with one of her friends.

She looks down at her feet, and she grins again. 'I went off to London. I thought maybe I'd get a job or something.'

She's supposed to be at school still, even if she never goes in.

'I met these guys. They were really nice. They said I could live in their squat for a bit.' She's really grinning now. 'Only there was a drug bust.'

'Who were they?' I don't like the thought of Tara living in some nasty flat with a load of druggy people.

'It's okay, Alex. They were really nice, honest.'

I screw up my face. I don't know.

'The police took me back to the station, kept me in a cell for hours. I was freezing. They were all right though.'

I'm scared for Tara on her own in a police station in London all night. I don't like it. 'What happened then? Were you arrested?'

She grins. Grins like she's not the sort of girl anyone can pin down. 'Nah,' she says. 'They questioned me for hours. I didn't tell them anything. When they found out my age they were quite nice really. Two of them escorted me to Paddington and put me on the train back here. They watched till it left the station so I couldn't get off.'

I'm not stupid. I think they were nice. Tara thinks it's funny but I think they saved her.

'What are you going to do now?' I'm getting twitchy because my lunch hour's nearly up and I feel really exposed, up on the field.

'I'm going to stay with my mate, Sharon. We'll get a flat together as soon as we can. I can sign on.'

'You haven't left school yet.'

She makes a face. 'I can soon. I'll be sixteen in a few months and I can do what I want. Anyway, are you okay?'

'Yeah, course,' I say. 'I'm at Granddad's. He's nice.'

She looks grey, and really old, all of a sudden. 'Not great, is it?'

'It's okay.' I run back down the field and into class. I'm late.


The next morning my form teacher looks round our class. She looks at me. 'Alex, can you please go to Mr Anderson's office at break-time today?'

I nod 'yes' at her.

Someone saw me then. My face feels hot.


Jez and Liam walk to Mr Anderson's office with me. I knock at the door but he doesn't answer. We wait outside. Him and the Head do this. They think you'll crack while you're waiting.

Jez and Liam look at me. Jez says, 'D'you think he's in there?'

There's a creak, footsteps, and the door opens.

Mr Anderson stands there, filling the whole door frame, scowling out at me.

'Marshall,' he says. His voice booms out. It makes me duck.

He looks at Jez and Liam. 'What are you boys doing here? Run along. This has nothing to do with you.'

I feel like I've got a stone stuck in my throat. Liam and Jez don't go. They stand one on each side of me. I can feel them looking at Mr Anderson as if they're daring him to be mean to me. I love Jez and Liam for that.

Mr Anderson's face changes. He looks nicer. 'Alex,' he says. He says it quite softly. 'Would you like to step inside? There may be something you'd like to talk to me about.'

I wasn't expecting him to be nice. I can't help it but I feel water swim round my eyeballs. Oh no. I blink hard.

'Come in,' he says and stands aside for me to walk through.

Jez and Liam stare. Liam winks at me and smiles to mean, 'Good luck, mate.'

Mr Anderson closes the door. It's just him and me now.

'Alex.' He doesn't take his eyes off me. 'Do you smoke?'

'No, Sir.'

'I'm glad to hear it.' He sits down in his seat, still staring. He looks like he's playing a game with me. 'I understand you were seen yesterday lunchtime at the cricket pavilion. With a girl.'

So that's it. He thinks I met a girlfriend up there. I can relax now.

'That was my sister, Sir. She'd got into some trouble in London. She just got back and she came to see me.'

'Couldn't she tell you when you got home?'

'Er, no, Sir.' I shift about a bit. 'We're not really at home at the moment, Sir.'

He sits forward and leans on his desk. 'What do you mean, you're 'not really at home?''

I can't tell him. I can't tell anyone. I don't know why. I just can't. I have to say something.

'Er, things are a bit difficult at the moment, Sir. I'm staying with my Granddad and my sister's staying with friends.'

I'm blinking back the wateriness really fast so I must look like I'm flickering. He stares at me, but his stare is different. Like he knows something. Or thinks he knows something.

'Would you like to talk about it?' His voice is quite soft.

I nearly do. I nearly vomit it all out, all of it, all the scared-ness, and the sick-ness, and the feeling on my own-ness, but I don't. I swallow it down again. He's the Deputy Head. I can't talk to him about private stuff.

I almost can. No, I can't.

He sits back in his chair. Watches me. I'm still blinking.

'Okay, Alex.' He gets up, walks to the door and opens it for me.

Liam and Jez are still outside. It's nice of them, but I don't want to see anyone right now. I want to be on my own.

Liam laughs and punches me, 'You're such a faker. You even had tears in your eyes.'

I grin at him and make a face like I'm really smart, 'Yeah, I had him fooled.'

Now I'm lying to my friends.


I stay with my granddad for a few weeks. He wakes me up in the morning but I'm not tired here.

Mum comes round one day. She looks upset. 'We all have to go home, Alex.'

I tell her I don't want to. 'I like it here. I can stay with Granddad.'

Her hands are all shaky. 'Your dad will have you and Tara put in care if we don't go back.' She's not looking at me. 'He says the family has to stay together.'

# 19

It's weird being home again. My mum's got a sour face most of the time. She's brought one of the beds down from the room she used to share with my dad, one of the ones that was pushed together. She's cleared out the shed downstairs near the front door and set it up in there. It's only got breeze block walls in the shed, but she's put a rug on the floor and some curtains up at the window, so it looks quite nice really.

She's got her single bed, a little cupboard with a lamp on top, an alarm clock, and she's brought down a chest of drawers. It's only the walls look funny. 'I can paint them and they won't look so bad.' She smiles like it's going to be okay.

She's down there and my dad's in their old room. It's all right for a few days.

I come in the front door and there he is. I've seen his face in all kinds of horrible ways but not as horrible as this. It's purply red, partly effort and partly anger, and his jaw is grinding. He's struggling upstairs with my mum's bed from the shed under one arm like it's a surfboard, and he's swearing and muttering all sorts of filthy stuff.

'Greg, please.' My mum's standing at the bottom of the stairs, staring up at him, watching him carry her bed up and round the bend in the stair. He has a hell of a job with it. It jams in the turn and he curses some more.

I look at my mum and I can't make out what she's thinking. She looks really mad but she looks really scared at the same time. Then she looks like she gives in.

I can hear him in his room. He bangs and crashes through their bedroom door and smashes the bed down on the wooden floor. 'There!' he shouts. 'That's where it should be.'

He comes back down for the mattress. My mum's gone in the kitchen. I go in with her and her face is red like it's stained blotchy.

'What are you going to do?' I say.

'There's nothing I can do. We're married. That's it.' She sounds really tired.

I have to stay awake at night. I have to make sure nothing bad is happening.

I sit on my bed. It's best to keep my clothes on. I need to be ready to jump out if I hear anything.

While I sit there, I imagine how I will kill him. I imagine him hurting my mum and I imagine me coming up behind him, holding a great huge knife in the air and plunging it deep into his back.

I have to make him stop.


My mum takes Scally to see the Vet. Mum fancies the vet. He's nice, really quiet and gentle. Scally hates him. He's whining and kicking up. Mum's got make up on. And perfume. I don't know how she can fancy the vet when he's just had his hand up Scally's bum. He's just different from my dad, that's all.


I don't do anything wrong at school anymore. I've grown out of that stupid stuff. I don't bother anyone. I just get in trouble for doing nothing.

The teachers say, 'Pull your socks up, Alex. You're almost at the bottom of the class. You can do better than that. It's not good enough, is it?' I don't know. I don't care really.

The teachers say they don't like the look on my face. I can't help my face.

I get in trouble for looking out of the window. I get in trouble for yawning. I can't help it if I'm tired.

Mum's in the dining room, sitting at the table staring out to sea. She doesn't hear me come in. I make her a cup of tea and sit down with her. She smiles at me. She looks nice when she smiles.

'Not too good is it?' she says.

I just make a face. I don't know what to say. It seems like we're stuck with it. I also know that she's here because she's keeping us from being put In Care. Maybe Tara and me would be better In Care so she doesn't have to stay.

'I don't think I can stick it.' She stares out of the window. 'He makes me. He makes me even though I try and push him off.'

I know what she's trying to say. I really don't want to hear this but I can't stick my fingers in my ears because that would be rude. I sit there and feel my face and neck burn hot because I have to hear it and I can't unhear it.

Her voice sounds like someone else's, all chewed up and twisted around, and she spits the words out like they taste bad. 'He says I'm his wife and I have to.' She's staring way off into the distance, to where the horizon is, way off out to sea, way away from here.

I can't run away either. I have to stay and look out for her.

## 20

No-one's home. I'm lying on the floor in front of our gas fire in the dining room, on the mat with Scally. He's warm. It's nice.

I hear the black gate screech and bang open. I wake up with my heart thumping. It must be my dad. He comes back sometimes.

I take off through the kitchen so I can get to the stairs before he gets in the front door. I can hear his boots on the steps outside as I run upstairs. I only just make it to my room. I don't notice the dark this time. I have to get to my room that's all.

I only just make it into bed, with all my clothes on still, and my door opens. I pull the covers up under my chin.

He sticks his face round my door. It looks all twisty and horrid. 'Where's your mother.' It doesn't sound nice how he says it.

'She's out with Auntie Sarah.'

'What are you doing still up, with the light on?'

I tell another lie. 'I was reading. I didn't know it was late.'

He doesn't answer, just shuts the door, and goes away. I can hear him moving stuff about downstairs. I stay awake for ages. He didn't see I was still dressed or I'd have been for it.

I get out of my clothes quick, in case he comes back. He doesn't.

I hear a funny murmuring noise. It's morning but it's really early, still half dark. I have to wake up some more so I can hear properly.

Mum's saying my name, but so softly I can hardly hear her. She's murmuring it.

I go outside my door. The door to Mum and Dad's room opposite mine is shut. Tara's door is shut too. The hall is dark. It's all quiet.

I hear the murmuring again.

It's coming from the box room next to the bathroom.

Something feels wrong. I don't like it.

I creep along the narrow hallway, down the two steps to the bathroom.

I push open the door to the box room, very slowly. I can feel someone in here.

She murmurs again. I'm glad it's Mum. Even though she doesn't sound right, I'm glad it's her.

I take a step into the room and lean round the door. It's too dark to see properly. She's lying on a narrow camp bed thing and, even though I can't see her, I know something bad has happened.

I go closer and look down at her. I don't know why she doesn't move. She knows I'm here though.

She tries to move one of her hands. 'Alex. You have to get the doctor.' She whispers it so quiet, I have to strain to get the words.

'What's the matter?' I whisper too. I don't know why we're whispering. I just know we have to.

'Phone the doctor, Alex. Tell him to come.'

'What is it?' But I can see now. She looks terrible. Her face is all red and the wrong shape. Her hair's a mess. She can't talk properly. Then she retches.

I jump back. 'What's happened? What's wrong? Can I get you some water or something?' I'm looking down at her as she tries to move her head. I don't know what to do. I've never seen my mum all weak and feeble.

She tries to look at me but she keeps putting her hand over her eyes. 'Your dad,' she mumbles. 'He hit me. A lot. Please get the doctor, Alex.'

I catch hold of her hand. 'I'll get him. He won't be long. Promise.' I say. I'm about to run off but she starts murmuring again.

'You'll have to be quiet, so he doesn't hear you.'

He's still here. In the house.

'He said I mustn't call you. He said he'd kill me.'

I stand there and stare at her.

'When I fell down he made me get up. Then he knocked me down again.' It doesn't sound like her voice.

'He hit me in the head and face. Just my head and face.'
It feels like we're the only two people in the whole world.

Until I step out into the hallway.

The bedroom doors are still shut. There's no sound. I need to get down the stairs without them making their creaking noise. I've got bare feet and I'm not heavy and I know which boards make the biggest creaks.

I get down the stairs without too much noise, but my heart is pumping so hard it feels like it's going to burst up out of my throat.

I open the kitchen door. There's no sign of Scally. I find the big telephone book and look for the number. I don't know it. We never need the doctor.

The kitchen joins into the dining room and the phone is on the worktop. If I pick up the phone, the other one - the one right next to my dad's head upstairs, will make a little ping noise. He will hear it.

I stand by the phone. I've got my hand over it. I'm afraid to pick it up. The house is so silent. The ping noise will be really loud next to his head. If he wakes up, what will I do?

I have to try.

I pick up the receiver, very slowly. I don't know why. It doesn't make any difference. It's still going to make a ping noise by his head if I pick it up quick or slow. I pick it up and hold it for a bit, listen into it to see if it clicks his end, if he's heard me.

I can't hear anything. The house is still quiet. He can be quiet too, for all that he's so big. I'm watching the kitchen door but I don't know what I'll do if he comes in.

I dial the number. It rings and rings. It rings for a long time. It's not quite light yet.

I'm watching the door. I'm thinking, 'Pick up the phone. Pick up the phone.' It stops ringing. A woman answers. She sounds cross. Now I have to speak. Out loud.

91

I whisper into the mouthpiece.

'I can't hear you. Speak up.'

I whisper again, 'Can I speak to Dr Gibson please?' I hate this woman.

'He's asleep. Who is this?'

'Marshall. Alex Marshall. My mum's ill. Can I speak to the doctor please?'

'What's wrong with your mother?' She sounds even crosser now.

I don't know what to say. I can't say what my dad's done. He might be listening on the extension. He might be outside the kitchen door. I think I'm going to cry. This horrid woman's not going to make me cry. I have to tell her something. I think she's going to put the phone down on me if I don't.

'She's got a bad head,' I say.

'A headache? What sort of headache?' She sighs and sounds like she thinks I'm simple or something. 'Give her an aspirin,' she says and puts down the phone.

I listen but I can't hear him moving upstairs. I'm freezing in my thin night stuff and bare feet. I phone again.

'It's really bad,' I say. 'She needs a doctor. It's not a headache. It's really bad.'

She sighs again, asks for my address. I tell her where we live but she says my house doesn't exist. I don't know why she's being so nasty. She must think I'm playing a trick on her.

I'm getting cross now, but I'm still whispering.

I have to describe everything to her, how the road goes, where the black gate is in the wall, the steps down to the house, everything.

She says he'll come.

I creep back upstairs to see if Mum's okay. She's still alive.

I wait with her. The house stays quiet. She mumbles that the room is spinning round and round. She retches again. I get her a flannel and a bowl from the bathroom.

I wait for ages. It's getting light. I don't think the doctor's coming.

I have to go down and phone again, pick up the phone again, make the upstairs phone ping next to his head again. I'm angry now though.

This time I speak to the woman in a different voice. 'Where's the doctor?'

'He's just having his breakfast,' she says.

'Having his breakfast?' I say. I know this horrid woman is stopping him from coming out. 'Tell him to hurry.'

He comes. I'm still in my night stuff. He's in a suit. He's got a bag. I whisper hello, let him in and creep upstairs on my toes with him behind me. I open the door to the box room and leave him to it. Then I zip into my room and get some clothes on while they're busy.

He comes out and I meet him in the hallway. I pull him back downstairs because I can see he's going to speak and I can't let him talk, not there, right near my dad sleeping.

We're by the front door and he turns to me. 'I need to call an ambulance.'

I nearly burst into tears right there. No. He can't pick up that phone again.

But he doesn't ask for the phone. 'I didn't realise how badly hurt your mother is. I would have come sooner.' He goes out of the front door. 'An ambulance will be here shortly.'

I go back upstairs and I hear movement in the hallway. My dad. My dad's in the box room.

I step in there. I go right past him. I go near my mum. I don't even look at him.

She murmurs something. I look up and he's standing there, looking down at her. He looks all saggy. I don't speak to him. Tara comes in. She starts yelling at him and he doesn't answer her. He just stands there looking saggy. Then he says, 'I'm sorry.' He sounds pathetic.

I hear the gate bang, noises outside on the steps, and I go down to the front door. It's two ambulance men. They take one look at our stairs and say they can't use a stretcher. They go back outside again.

They come back, tell me they've got a special folding chair they can use. I wait at the bottom of the stairs. They come down very slowly with Mum sort of sitting up. Now it's daylight I can see her face looks really mashed, like a boxer. I hang about. I don't know what to do with myself.

I follow them outside and up the steps to the road. They struggle around getting her onto a bed in the back of the ambulance. They put straps on her to hold her down. Then she retches and they have to take the straps off so she can be sick again.

One of them looks at me. 'You can come too, if you like.'

Tara's out in the road now. She's got her arms all wrapped round herself like she's cold. 'I'll stay here.' She's really pale and she looks small.

I get in the back and sit on a little seat. One man stays beside my mum and keeps an eye on her. It's really horrible.

At the hospital the doctors take Mum away and I sit by an empty bed for a long time. It's very quiet here. After a while a nurse walks past. She stops and looks back at me as if she didn't expect anyone to be sitting there.

'Would you like a cup of tea?' She speaks to me gently, like she's kind.

She brings it in a cup and saucer. It's not hot. Nice of her though.

## 21

When my mum wakes up, she talks really quietly. She says the front door was locked so she couldn't get in. She tried and tried the door but it was bolted from the inside, so she had to come round the front to the house, by the sea, and try to get in the garden door.

The house was all pitch black and quiet. She opened the door from the garden and stepped into the sitting room. It was so dark she couldn't see. She was half way across it when he spoke to her from out of the armchair. He was waiting for her.

He got up and caught hold of her.

She says he told her not to call my name. He said if she called my name he'd kill her. She called for me anyway and he hit her harder. I feel bad I didn't hear her. If I'd heard and come down he might have stopped.

She starts to tell me how he was only hitting her in the head and face, that he said he wanted to ruin her good looks forever. That he was going to kill her anyway. She cries then.

She might just as well have yelled for me.

I imagine him sitting waiting in the dark, listening to her trying the front door, waiting while she walked round outside the house, hearing her feet crunching on the gravel.

I imagine him waiting while she opened the garden door, watching her walk across the sitting room.

I don't get how he could sit there all quiet in the dark and then jump up and get her.

She says he put her to bed on the floor of the box room. She said he wanted to do it to her after. My eyes bug out. I don't like it that she tells me stuff like this. I think they're weird enough. I don't want to know about that stuff.

I don't like it that she's crying. I don't know what we're going to do now.

My Auntie Sarah comes to the hospital to get me. She takes me to my granddad's and drops me off outside his flat. 'I'm sorry, Alex. Your dad's my brother; I can't get involved. I hope you understand.'

She's got my school clothes in a bag. 'I won't be able to see any of you. It's a bit difficult for me.'

So I won't see Ryan anymore.

I have to call round and see Tommy. I tell him my dad's gone mad and bashed up my mum. I tell him not to tell anyone. Tommy won't tell.

I like it at my granddad's. He doesn't ask me anything. We get along just fine.

The doctors fix Mum up and she comes to get me one day. She whispers all the time. It's hard to hear her. 'We're going away. To your aunt's, near London.'

She means forever. I can hear it in her voice.

I don't want to leave my friends. I like it at school. I don't know anyone in London. I bet they fight in their schools. No-one fights in mine. Everyone's nice.

She starts crying. Says she can't bear it. 'I can't stay here, Alex. Will you come, please?'

I leave her whispering with her old dad and go round to Tommy's.

I tell him I've got to leave but he mustn't tell anyone what's up. I get him to say I've gone away for a few months because I've done something wrong, to a young offenders place or something. I don't want anyone to know what my family's like.

'I'll write you letters sometimes,' I say, 'tell you what it's like.'

I know I'll hate it.

I feel better being with Tommy, even though today he doesn't look too cheerful. He's my mate.

On the way back to my granddad's I think maybe I won't really need to go to a school up there. Maybe we'll just be there for a week or two and I can come back, be with my friends again.

When I get there, Mum's got her coat on. 'Are you ready then?' She looks grim, and scared too. 'We have to go back to the house.'

'What for? I don't want to go back there.' I don't care that I've only get one set of clothes.

She sits down. 'Alex, It'll be okay. I know some of the policemen here. They've been very kind. They're going to come with us.' She looks at her watch. 'I need to get some things.'

The police are going to come with us. Like that's not going to attract attention or anything. What if he's in there? Will they all get into a fight?

Tara doesn't come. Mum and me drive along the main road. It looks spooky along there. I hate the whole road. She keeps the doors locked till the police car comes.

Two policemen get out. My mum gets out and stands near to them. I can't hear what they're saying but they look over at me. She nods her head for me to get out of the car so I do as I'm told.

I don't want to go near that black door in the wall. I don't want to go down those steps.

One of the policemen goes first. He turns to me. 'We can't come inside the house, we're not allowed to do that, but we'll wait outside and watch to see that you're okay.'

Great. So we'll get inside. My dad'll jump out and kill us both and they'll catch him after. That's dumb.

We all go down the steps, really slowly, one at a time, like we're feeling our way. The first policeman goes up and rings the bell. Mum and me stand well back. I'm ready to run. There's no answer. He tries the door. It's locked.

Mum gets out her key. It doesn't work. The locks are different.

The other policeman says, 'You might have to break in.' He shuffles his feet about in the gravel. 'I didn't say that, I just thought it.'

Seems a funny time to be making a joke.

We go round the front, by the garden door. It's locked from the inside.

I say the only way in's through the sitting room window. One window never shuts properly and I can get my hand in and loosen the catch. We don't have to break anything then.

I still think he's in there, hiding. And I don't want him to hear the glass breaking.

The garden's all overgrown. It looks like nobody cares, and it's very quiet. My voice sounds really loud. Even though the sun's shining I'm scared. I've got stomach ache.

I get my fingers inside and feel for the catch. I get it loose from the hook and, as I pull the window open, the metal arm that holds open the window falls hard onto the sill with a big echoey crash. I jump. My heart is pumping. I think he's in the sitting room, waiting. Waiting for us. In the dark.

I hang back. The tallest policemen says, 'There you go. Can you climb in there? You're only small aren't you? Do you want a leg up?'

I probably can climb in there. I still don't want to. I'm not sure what I'm going to fetch from my room but I think I can live without it.

Mum's up close to me. 'C'mon, Alex. It'll be okay. He's not here.'

I don't know how she knows that.

The tall policemen bends forward and holds out his linked hands so I can step on them and climb in.

I'm half way in. The sitting room looks strange. Empty. But the air inside is full of something. I really don't want to get off the sill.

I stay there for ages, half in and half out. It hurts my leg. I have to stay there and listen to the air, feel if he's in there.

The tall policemen says, 'Are you okay, lad?'

I turn and look at him. He looks okay. He's sound. I drop inside the window onto the floor.

Mum climbs in after me. She has a bit of a struggle squeezing through the little window.

I cross the room. It seems a really long way to the door.

I open it and look into the dark hallway. It's black. There's no sound.

I can feel Mum behind me. 'Go on, Alex. We'll just run upstairs and grab some stuff, okay? Be quick?'

The stair creaks when I put my foot on it. She's breathing right behind me.

We go up. It seems like every stair creaks, like it's trying to tell us something. Like it's complaining.

The two doors are shut, their room and mine. She turns the handle and pushes open her door, and I go into my room.

I feel sad when I step in there. All my stuff's still lying around – my books, toys I had when I was a kid, my radio. My bed's all rumpled like someone's been sleeping in it but there aren't any sheets, just blankets in a mess.

When I open the drawer next to my bed and put my hand in there's something crusty and rubbery in there, like a big dry splat of something. It's dried up sick. I pull my hand out quick. Why would someone be in my room and throw up in my drawer?

I look back at my bed and wonder who's been in it. There's a blood stain on the mattress. I think this is a girl's period but I don't know how it got in my bed.

It's not my room anymore.

I pull a few things out of the clothes drawer and unplug my radio, pick up a few books and stuff them in my backpack. I leave everything else.

The policemen are still waiting outside the sitting room window. I smile at them. I'm okay now. The sun's out.

When we get up to the road Mum says to them she'll call by the station on the way. She talks fast like she hasn't got enough air.

We go back to my granddad's to say goodbye. 'You're a good boy, Alex.' he says and he musses my hair. 'Look after your mum.'

We drive to the Police Station and the two nice policemen come out and get in their car. Mum looks terrified. When she pulls away from the kerb, their car pulls away too. I look back at them.

Mum grips the steering wheel and looks in her mirror. 'They're coming with us.'

'Why?' I think I know. I'm glad too.

'They can't come all the way. They're not allowed. They're going to escort us to the edge of their boundary. Then, we're in another police area so they can't follow us there.'

She thinks he's going to come after us. That's why she's hardly breathing.

She drives quite slowly. Keeps looking in her mirror. The police car's still there. It's there all the way to the edge of the county. Then she stops and gets out.

She goes behind the car and talks to the policemen. I get out and say thank you as well.

We're on our own now.

I miss Scally.

22

It doesn't work out at the new school. I like the look of some of the kids but no-one likes me. I just keep to myself.

We've been living with my aunt for about four months now. She's nice but I don't belong here.

Tara came up on the train early on. She stayed for a couple of days, made a fuss and went back. She wants to be with her friends. She's sixteen now so she's got herself a bed-sit somewhere back home.

'I can go back too,' I say to Mum. 'I can live with Tara in her bed-sit.'

Mum doesn't want me to go back. She wants us to go and live somewhere new, where we don't know anybody. I don't like not knowing anybody. She gets really upset about it. My aunt says I can't go home to my town; she says my mum needs me.

I feel bad that I want to leave my mum here, but this isn't my place. I want to be in the place I know.

## 23

That was stupid of me. I thought we could come back and I could be with my friends again, carry on like before. But it feels different. It's like while I've been away everything's changed. I feel a bit awkward. When I see my mates I don't know what to say. They seem really young, and a bit silly. Tommy's all right but it's not the same, even with him.

Mum and me are living in a different town now. There's no beach, just lots of traffic. It's great to have Scally back though. Old Bill next door kept an eye on him while we were gone. He's really old now, ninety-eight in dog years, but he's still my best mate. I take him to the playing field. He sniffs other dog's wee all round the edges and then cocks his leg on it even though nothing comes out. He seems quite happy doing that. The playing field's okay.

The flat we're renting is really small. We share the kitchen and the bathroom with some other people. It's upstairs above an undertakers. He's a nice undertaker, but still.

My dad had to go to court for what he did to my mum. He's on the front page of the newspaper again. His face, his name.

I went hot all over when I saw what they'd written. In big black capitals. There, for everyone to see.

MAN TRIES TO MAKE LOVE TO WIFE AFTER HE NEARLY
KILLED HER

I feel sick.

It's Friday, so I go over to the youth club, see who's about. I haven't seen anyone for a bit, but they're just kids in there, giggling and shoving around.

I go up the steps into Martin's little music box. I like Martin. He smiles at me. 'How you doin'?' he says, as he changes the music over. 'Nice to see you back.'

'I'm all right, mate. Just thought I'd come in and say hello, y'know.'

'Yeah.' He takes off his headphones. 'I saw your dad in the paper.'

I don't like him knowing. I guess everyone knows.

I don't go to the club again.

## 24

There's an old pub down a lane on the edge of town. It's really old, over four hundred years. Awesome. It's got a thatched roof and everything. My mum's working there now so I go there instead. It's always full of happy people laughing. No-one's mean.

I collect up glasses and wash them for a bit of cash. My mum smiles all the time. She even gets asked out a few times.

The flat's really small. There's no room for Tara here but she likes it in her bed-sit anyway. She comes over for a bath and Sunday roast sometimes. It's nice. I'm still bottom of my class, but it's okay. Mum's happy. I'm happy. No-one ever shouts.

It's safe here.

# Note from the editor

Alex Marshall found school difficult, and didn't feel very sociable for a while. But he got through it, grew up, married, and had two children of his own. He says,

'It never occurred to me to talk to anyone about what was going on at home when I was growing up. I thought I was the only kid on the planet who was having a tough time of it. It's been good to talk about all that. I feel I can let it go now, put it all behind me.

'It's nice to have grown up and to have my own children. It's given me the opportunity to be the kind of dad that I wish my dad had been. We all choose how we behave in the end. I don't believe in excuses. Any adult scaring or hurting a child is plain wrong.

'My children are brilliant and my wife's wonderful. We look out for our kids, keep them safe, we have a lot of fun together and, … we leave the lights on at night if they want.'

'If there had been any helplines around back then, I could have phoned. It would have felt okay to talk to a stranger.'


No-one has to put up with violence in the home.

If you need to talk to someone about problems you're facing, or worries you've got, there are charities that can help but, for legal reasons, they cannot be listed here. Please look online or visit your local library for information.

# Notes on the author

Amanda Speedie writes short stories, features and film reviews and is working on a novel and a screenplay. She also writes business copy.

www.amandaspeedie.com

Printed in the United Kingdom by
Lightning Source UK Ltd., Milton Keynes
138844UK00001B/91/P